How I Ended Up Married to a Perfect Stranger

(Steve Cooper's Version of the Story)

Okay, so Eden Wells isn't *perfect*, exactly. But she *is* absolutely adorable, even when she's lying through her pretty little teeth. That's why, when I caught her snooping around the mansion we both wanted to win—totally against the rules, of course—I couldn't turn her in.

And that's also why I couldn't say no to this #%&! scheme of hers. See, she figured a husband and wife would have a better shot at winning this beautiful old house we both wanted, and...

And before I knew it, I was going along with this charade—and wondering just how many cold showers a man can take in one night. Especially when it's his *wedding* night....

Dear Reader,

I love my house. I realize that's an odd thing to say to start off a letter about romances, but…well, it's true. And it's also relevant. The minute I saw my house for the first time, I knew I had to have it. Luckily, I got it—and twelve and a half years later, I'm still happy there. Eden Wells, heroine of Lynda Simons' *The Wedding and the Little White Lie*, felt much the same when she first saw the big old mansion that was up for grabs in a local contest. And being married would make winning so much more likely. So she hooked up with fellow contestant Steve Cooper and…well, let's just say that I think Steve's the *real* prize. Read the book and you'll know just what I'm talking about.

And next up…*Big Bad Dad*, the latest from Yours Truly phenomenon Christie Ridgway. How *does* she keep coming up with winner after winner? I don't know, and so long as she keeps on doing it, I don't care! For Carly Carrothers, there's one cardinal rule in life: Never—but *never*—fall in love with a single dad. Especially when he's your boss. Especially when he's adamantly antimarriage. Especially—oh, forget it! She's hooked. And you will be, too, from the moment you read page one.

And don't forget: After you enjoy both of this month's books, come back again next month for two more great novels all about meeting—and marrying!—Mr. Right.

Yours,

Leslie J. Wainger
Executive Senior Editor

Please address questions and book requests to:
Silhouette Reader Service
U.S.: 3010 Walden Ave., P.O. Box 1325, Buffalo, NY 14269
Canadian: P.O. Box 609, Fort Erie, Ont. L2A 5X3

LYNDA
SIMONS

The Wedding and the Little White Lie

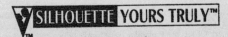

Published by Silhouette Books

America's Publisher of Contemporary Romance

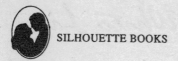

For Lorne,
Because that's what I'd be without him

SILHOUETTE BOOKS

ISBN 0-373-52074-3

THE WEDDING AND THE LITTLE WHITE LIE

Copyright © 1998 by Lynda Simmons

This edition published by arrangement with Harlequin Books S.A.

® and TM are trademarks of Harlequin Books S.A., used under license. Trademarks indicated with ® are registered in the United States Patent and Trademark Office, the Canadian Trade Marks Office and in other countries.

Printed in U.S.A.

From the author

Dear Reader,

"No, it doesn't make you look fat."

"The check's in the mail."

"I'm glad your mother's coming to visit. Really."

Little white lies. Everyone tells them: friends, lovers—and very clever husbands. According to mine, I haven't changed a bit since that sunny October afternoon when we finally took that stroll down the aisle. He smiles when he says it, and I smile when I hear it. And that's the beauty of the little white lie.

But what happens when a lie takes on a life of its own? When the Pinocchio Syndrome kicks in, and the whole thing just keeps getting bigger and bigger until you can't remember where it started or why. And worse still, you start to believe it yourself.

If you're smart, you tell the truth and duck low for a while.

But if you're an author, you turn it into a book.

Enjoy!

Lynda

Books by Lynda Simons

Yours Truly

Marrying Well
The Wedding and the Little White Lie

1

The sky was just beginning to lighten as Steve Cooper pulled his pickup into the curb. An old orange tom lounging on a nearby porch lifted his head, watching while Steve shut off the engine and rolled down the window. Finding nothing of interest in a face that was broad and dark and badly in need of a shave, the cat yawned once and went back to sleep.

Steve couldn't help smiling as he tapped a cigarette from the pack beside him. The cat was typical of most Devon Avenue residents—haughty, indifferent and overfed. And from what he'd seen so far, it looked as though nothing much had changed in the quiet Connecticut town of Kilbride.

Stepping out of the truck, he settled back against the cab, crossed one booted foot over the other and lit the cigarette, drawing the smoke in deeply while he tried to roll the kinks from his shoulders. After two straight days on the road, he was more than ready for a hot shower and cool sheets. But it wouldn't be long before Devon Avenue was wide-awake, and for now it was only him and the cat and the lady he'd come to see—which was exactly the way he wanted it.

Even in this light she was a beauty. Less spectacularly dressed than her wealthier sisters perhaps, but still possessing the same grace and dignity that would always set them apart from their jealous neighbors.

He knew a lot about the older two—their lives and loves, the comings and goings that had shaped what they were today. But this youngest was a puzzle. All he knew was that she had fallen on hard times in her prime, suffering years of abuse and neglect at the hands of the one man who should have loved her most, James T. Rusk—one of Kilbride's wealthiest sons and as big a fool as Steve had ever met.

He dropped the unfinished cigarette and crushed it beneath his heel. How anyone could treat a lady of her stature so callously was beyond his understanding. But then he'd always had a soft spot for grand old Victorian homes, and this one in particular.

Beneath the crumbling chimneys and rotted trim, she was a lovely three-tiered wedding cake—all Queen Anne turrets, pointed gables and a wraparound porch that had felt like home the first time he climbed the stairs. And after five years of waiting, she would finally be his. Reaching in through the open window of the truck, Steve picked up a letter from the dash:

Mrs. Dorothy Margaret Elson is pleased to announce that your entry has been selected as one of three finalists in the *Dreams of Devon Contest.*

The Kilbride Historical Board will be conducting interviews on June 3 at the Central Library on Wickham Street in Kilbride. Details as follows:

Steve shook his head as he tucked the page into his shirt pocket. Funny how things turned out sometimes. Here he'd spent years trying to get his hands on Rusk's house and now Dorothy Elson, sole heir to the estate, couldn't wait to get rid of it. And lucky for him, she'd decided not to sell after all. Instead Mrs. Elson was holding a contest.

For an entry fee of one hundred dollars and an essay entitled For The Love Of Devon, she was willing to give one thousand people a chance at home ownership, plus the $100,000 pot for restoration. The only thing the wealthy philanthropist wasn't willing to give them was a chance to see anything inside.

The windows were to remain boarded and the doors sealed until the winner was announced. Any breach of that condition would lead to automatic disqualification of the entrant. Her handwritten line at the bottom of the entry had pretty much summed it up: "Don't like the rules? Don't enter," which had suited Steve just fine. The fewer people who tried for his house, the better.

And now, the only thing standing in his way was the interview. One hour alone with three of the state's most committed restorationists—people who were bound to appreciate a man with talent, tools and a little time on his hands. A smile softened the corners of his mouth. It didn't get much better than this.

He crossed his arms over his chest and let his gaze drift slowly over the house. It was odd that of all the homes he'd seen over the years, this was the one that kept tugging him back. Yet there was no question that this was the house he would do for himself, taking his time and feeling his way, with no one to answer to and no one else to please. And when he was finished, nothing would ever persuade him to move again.

As he turned back to the truck, a flicker of light near the house caught his eye. Probably nothing more than a neighbor letting out an early-rising pet. But the morning was still new and sleep could wait a while yet. So he grabbed another cigarette and settled back against the cab, watching his house closely while the streetlights flickered and died.

Eden tucked the flashlight into her back pocket, blew her bangs out of her eyes and swung the crowbar up again. One nail was all that stood between her and the glass now. One stubborn, slightly out of reach nail, and time was running out.

As if to punctuate the thought, the first soft light of dawn touched the balcony above her, prompting every squawking bird in the yard to turn the volume up a notch in celebration. She glared at the trees, wishing again that she'd brought her cat along for the weekend then turned back to the window. It was now or never.

She glanced down at the weathered lid beneath her sneakers, hoping the old barrel would hold out a while longer, then she jammed the bar under the wood and jerked down hard. She sucked in a hissing breath as the barrel wobbled under her and silently cursed Mrs. Dorothy Margaret Elson and the ridiculous rule that made all of this necessary.

What possible harm could it do if a finalist took one quick look inside? Especially if that particular finalist knew for certain that she didn't stand a chance without it?

None at all, Eden decided, and put her shoulder to the bar. Not after what she'd learned last night. From that point on, all bets were off and it was every finalist for herself. And as long as she didn't get caught, things would work out just fine.

One final push and the nail gave way. Eden dropped the bar and slowly lowered the board to the ground. Heart pounding, she cast one last glance around the yard, then yanked the sleeve of her sweatshirt over her fist and rubbed the worst of the dirt from a circle of glass. Pulling the flashlight from her pocket, she drew in a deep breath, pressed the light to window and leaned in. A smile curved her lips. The house was as good as hers.

"Find anything interesting?"

Eden snapped around at the sound of a smooth, rich baritone. "Not really," she said, noting only that the intruder wasn't wearing a uniform before the barrel pitched forward.

She made a grab for the window, realizing too late there was no stopping it this time. The barrel rocked and she squeezed her eyes shut, waiting. But instead of the ground, she felt a pair of large, strong arms close around her, holding her tight and cushioning the fall as they tumbled to the ground.

Eden opened her eyes, but instead of rolling away she stayed where she was, cradled against him, aware of every contour, every point of pressure against her skin. Even through the heavy sweatshirt, she could feel the solid warmth and power in the arms that held her and the body behind her.

His breath was warm on her neck. "Are you all right?" he asked in that same smooth voice that had caused all the trouble in the first place.

That was all it took. "Fine," she said, rolling away and releasing the breath she hadn't realized she'd been holding. She wondered about that as she scrambled to her feet. About being motionless and breathless, and trying to remember if she'd ever been both at the same time.

Then again, breathless always went with nervous, and considering how much trouble this guy could be, she was definitely nervous. As for motionless? She'd think about that later. Right now, her biggest concern was getting herself out of there. Preferably without a police escort.

"I want to thank you," she said brightly and turned, only to find herself smiling at a shirt button. The second one to be exact—an unusual sensation for a woman accustomed to standing eye-to-eye with most men she met.

She lifted her gaze, meeting eyes so brown they were almost black, and a grin that was wide and white—and laughing at her.

Laughing was good, she decided. People who laughed weren't usually in a hurry to call police. Or the Historical Board. She took a quick step back. What she needed now was a good story. And an even better exit line. She tilted her head and flashed him a charming smile. "I suppose you're wondering what I'm doing here."

"I'm curious, yes," he said, then bent down to right the barrel, his movements surprisingly fluid and graceful for a man of his size.

More curious than nervous now, Eden stood back and studied him openly. He wasn't a man who would immediately be called handsome—his cheeks were too broad and his chin too narrow for that. But his eyes were perfect, heavy-lidded and fringed with thick, dark lashes, while his mouth was full and sensuous.

She'd figured him for a nosy neighbor at first, but now she wasn't so sure. There was nothing at all settled or domestic about him. Nothing to suggest he spent his Saturdays pushing a lawn mower or cruising garage sales. And he certainly didn't look like a member of any Historical Board she'd ever met.

If anything, the word that came to mind was *cowboy*. Not the aw-shucks, easy-to-handle kind, either. But the sexy, bad-boy type who always looks like he'd just rolled out of bed, and not necessarily his own. Which only confirmed what friends had been telling her for weeks: it was definitely time to go cold turkey on the country music videos again.

But if this cowboy wasn't a neighbor or a Board member, then who was he?

"So tell me about yourself," he said as he straightened and turned to her. "Starting with your name."

She looked up into his eyes and her mind went blank. She felt as if he was looking right through her, into her, yet his own dark gaze was completely unreadable. "Eden," she whispered, then blinked and moved to put some more distance between them. "Eden Wells."

She would have sworn something flickered in those eyes, but it was gone so fast she couldn't be sure.

He leaned a shoulder against the wall and folded his arms, making himself comfortable—as though he had all the time in the world and nowhere special to spend it. Which was too bad.

"So, Eden, what were you doing up on that barrel anyway?"

Realizing there was no way out of it, she struck an equally casual pose and hoped for the best. "It's all very simple, really. You see, I work in films. For a studio in New York."

She didn't see any reason to mention that the studio was really a computer station in her living room. Or that the films were really nothing more than flashy infomercials. So she left it at that and paused, hoping he'd take the bait the way most people did. Maybe ask if she'd worked with any of his favorite stars, tell her his Oscar choices—anything that would give her time to collect her thoughts. But he simply stood there watching her, and it occurred to her that he wasn't anything at all like most people.

"I focus on short pieces for the most part." She paused again, this time strictly for effect. And when she spoke again, she kept her voice low, secretive, seeing how it would work. "But this project is a little different."

He inclined his head slightly, his voice dropping to the same level as hers. "Go on."

She tried to keep from smiling. So he liked a mystery. Well now, she'd just have to see what she could come up with.

She tapped her fingertips together prayer style and bowed her head. "This film will be a sweeping epic, tracing a curse that dates back to the Revolutionary War. And this house..." She spread her arms wide, her voice rising as she hit on her story at last. "This house will be the opening scene."

Steve listened, wondering what she really did when she wasn't breaking into houses. She headed for the gazebo, still talking, and he fell into step beside her, willing to play along, to watch her for a while longer.

And she was magnificent to watch—tall and lithe, with ivory skin and the kind of red-gold hair that always looks best in the sunshine. While she might live in New York, there was a touch of country in that smoky voice. Which might explain why she looked so perfect standing there with the breeze in her hair and the smell of fresh grass all around her.

"It's a fascinating story," she continued. "And all the more compelling because it's based on truth...."

She was quick, too, he gave her that. But not quick enough.

When he'd first spotted her up on that barrel, her nose pressed against the glass like a little girl, he'd assumed she was a very inexperienced thief. But as soon as she'd told him who she was, he knew she was casing the house for different reasons altogether.

Eden Wells. Who could forget a name like that? Especially when he'd read it a hundred times since the letter arrived. She was the competition.

She looked up at him, those blue eyes holding his gaze a moment before moving on. "At first, everything seems so innocent..."

Innocent? Not likely. And not really blue, either, he decided. More the soft, hazy gray of the sky where it meets the horizon. And every once in a while those eyes would slant in his direction, trying to gauge how much more it would take to get rid of him.

"So naturally, when I saw that one of the windows was exposed, curiosity got the best of me—"

"The board was off when you got here?"

She looked over at him. "Vandalism," she said solemnly, then sighed. "There's no escaping it."

Steve shook his head in admiration. Damn, she was good.

She gave him a tiny smile. "But it's getting late. I shouldn't hold you up any longer, Mr...."

"No problem," Steve said. "So what do you think of the house?"

Her smile dimmed a little, realizing he wasn't ready to let her off the hook yet. "Very interesting. The trim, the towers—"

"I meant inside."

She shrugged and glanced up at the house. "I don't know. You made your entrance before I had time to see anything."

"Maybe I can make things up to you." Steve walked over to the barrel, picked up the flashlight and carried it back to her. "Go ahead. Take a look."

Eden moistened her lips and stared at him, trying to figure the risk. His eyes were still unreadable, but if he was going to report her, wouldn't he have said something by now? Besides, how could anyone smile like that and not be trusted? And how could she pass up the chance?

"Thanks." She grabbed the light and sprinted back to the barrel, all thoughts of getting rid of him forgotten as she hoisted herself up.

"Let me help," he said, holding the barrel steady.

She grinned at him then pushed the flashlight against the glass and turned it on, moving the beam slowly while her eyes grew accustomed to the faint glow.

"What do you see?" he asked.

"High ceilings, stained glass." She wrinkled her nose. "Godawful wallpaper."

He laughed. "Anything else?"

She cupped a hand around her eyes. Moldings, carvings—everything she'd been reading about packed into one room, confirming what she'd suspected all along: poor taste knew no class barriers. But it did give her the edge she needed for the interview.

She handed him the flashlight. "I see a strong William Morris influence, and a definite tendency to wretched excess."

"I take it you're not a fan of Victoriana."

"I'm trying. But I have to admit, I can't help thinking that Norman Bates' mother is in there somewhere." She planted her feet and got ready to jump.

"Oh, no," he said, and wrapped his arms around her waist. "While the thought of rolling around on the grass with you again does have its appeal, I don't think I could take another crash landing."

Before she could object, he was lifting her off and setting her down in front of him. His hands rested lightly on her hips while his mouth slowly curved. "Better?"

She looked up into his eyes and could only nod. So she dropped her gaze and took a step back. She would definitely have to think about this motionless thing sometime soon. "Thanks for your help," she said. "It will make all the difference to my work."

He bowed his head. "Anything for art."

Eden scooped up her bag and swung it over her shoulder. "It was nice to meet you, Mr...."

"The pleasure was mine." He reached down and picked up the crowbar. "Don't forget this."

Her eyes widened. "Oh, that's not mine."

"Ah, yes. Vandals." He saw her cheeks pinken. She really didn't lie very well at all, he thought, and was surprised that it should please him so much.

"Goodbye, Mr...."

He held out a hand. "Cooper. Steve Cooper."

He felt her fingers tighten as her face registered surprise, then horror. "Dreams of Devon," he continued, drawing out the moment, confirming the worst. "I'm a finalist." He turned her hand over, placed the bar into her palm and closed her fingers around it. "And you, I believe, are in a lot of trouble."

2

He watched her jaw tighten. "So are you going to tell the Board?"

Steve smiled. He should have known she wouldn't waste time mincing words. "Is that what you'd do?"

She lifted one shoulder, let it fall. Almost casual, as though nothing mattered. But he could see the tension in the way she gripped the strap of that huge bag. "It would depend."

"On what?"

"On how much I wanted that house."

"And how much is that?"

She looked at him, her gaze level and direct. "Enough to deny every word of it."

The determination in her eyes had him wondering more than it should have, more than he wanted it to.

"So will you tell them?" she demanded again, watching him closely.

He was tempted to say yes, to make her sweat a little longer, but instead he said, "I haven't decided."

She tilted her head to the side. "Can I possibly persuade you not to?"

He took a step closer, wondering just how far she'd go. "What did you have in mind?"

She raised her chin. "How much would it take?"

He laughed and moved forward, backing her against the wall. "There's only one thing that would persuade me, Eden."

He enjoyed the way her eyes widened. "And what would that be?"

He bent to her, letting his lips brush her ear, smiling to himself when she trembled ever so slightly. "The truth," he whispered, then turned and headed for the gazebo.

He sat down on the steps and leaned into the corner, stretching his legs out while she caught up. She stood in front of him, hands on her hips, eyes narrowed and deadly. "Do you enjoy making a fool of everyone, or is it just me?"

He smiled up at her. "I'd have to say it's just you. Look, we both know you've been lying since the moment I got here, but if you tell me the truth about what you're doing here, I might be willing to forget the whole incident."

She stood a moment longer, the very picture of righteous indignation. Then her shoulders slumped and she dropped her bag on the ground. "All right, you win." She shoved his legs over and sat down. "To be honest, I never expected to be a finalist. A friend showed me the flyer so I entered. It was a spur-of-the-moment thing."

"A crumbling house you decided you wanted on the spur of the moment?"

She nodded then bent to pluck a fluffy dandelion from a clump beside the step. "Anyway, when the letter came, I made up my mind to win. However, there was the problem of the Historical Board and the fact that I knew nothing about Victorian architecture."

She held the weed to her lips and blew gently, a smile curving her lips as the delicate seeds danced through the air, obviously mindless of the fact that she had just condemned every lawn for blocks to a sea of tiny golden heads in the spring.

"After weeks of research, I now know every term, every style, every major architect and decorator of that era."

"Very impressive," Steve offered.

The smile dimmed as she tossed the stem aside. "I thought so, too. But last night, I found out it wasn't going to be enough to win. So I wandered over, noticed a loose board on the window and took it as a sign that Dorothy Elson's rule was not meant for me." She looked over at him. "And you know the rest."

But he wanted to know more. "Then there's no sweeping epic?"

She sat back, her elbows resting on the stair behind. "It's more of a brief anecdote, but it will still be wonderful."

"Then you really are a filmmaker?"

"I told you so, didn't I?"

Her wounded expression made him smile. "You told me a lot of things."

"Well, that much was true. Only they're not the kind you're probably thinking about. I make commercial videos. Training tapes, industrial brochures. Award winners, too, I might add."

"And will I have seen any of these award winners of yours?"

"Perhaps." She gave him a thoughtful look. "I did some groundbreaking work on kiwis last year. Held them spellbound in the produce aisle."

She rose and stood before him. "Picture a line of shopping carts in front of one tiny monitor. The shoppers are quiet, the cash registers are quiet, even the kids are quiet. Suddenly the tape rolls. All eyes shift to the screen, everyone breathless as 'Kiwi—Plain and Small' begins." She closed her eyes. "It was very moving."

"I'm shivering."

She laughed as she sat down beside him. "So was every-one else, but only because the monitor was too close to the freezers. However, I'm told the sales of kiwis jumped dramatically that month."

"Is that why you do it? To sell kiwis?"

She looked down at her hands. "We all have to sell something."

She said it so quickly, so automatically, Steve figured it had to be a stock answer, one she had given too often, making him wonder what the real answer was. And letting him know it was definitely time to go.

She turned to him. "So what do you think? Does the window incident stay between us?"

He got to his feet. "It always would have."

Her smile was warm, genuine. "Thanks. I appreciate it."

He grinned at her. "Don't, because if you'd been a serious threat, I might have reacted differently."

She was right beside him when he headed for the driveway. "What is that supposed to mean?"

Steve stopped, figuring he owed her at least that. "Think about it, Eden. The Historical Society is making the final decision. What do you think their main concern will be?"

"History, perhaps?"

"Architecture," he said blandly. "Have you read their mandate?"

"Every word."

He tried not to show his surprise. Underestimating Eden Wells would definitely be a man's downfall. "Then you know that these are people concerned with preserving and restoring old buildings. It won't take them long to discover you know nothing practical about the process."

"And you do, of course."

He pulled a card from his pocket and handed it to her.

"'Cooper Construction,'" she read then looked up at him. "You're a builder?"

"Who specializes in the restoration and re-creation of historic homes. And just so there are no hard feelings, if you ever do make a sweeping epic, I promise you can use the house for the opening shot. No crowbar required." He started walking again. "How does that sound?"

"Premature," she said with enough conviction to make him stop and turn around. She ran back to the gazebo and picked up her bag. "Do you know what I have in here?"

"A chain saw, perhaps?"

She gave him a patient smile as she strolled toward him. "Besides that." Reaching into the bag, she lifted out a slender binder and presented it to him. "Footloose Video Productions proudly presents, 'Kilbride, The Movie.' And believe me, it's going to be another award winner."

Steve honestly tried not to laugh. "You have to be kidding."

"Not at all," she said matter-of-factly. "Extensive market research shows that the town of Kilbride is sadly lacking in any kind of visual presentation for trade and tourism shows, so I know they'll be interested. Especially when I tell them I'll produce the video at my own cost, provided I win the house, of course."

"Sounds like bribery."

Her smile could only be described as cocky. "I prefer to think of it as Mutually Beneficial Encouragement."

"You would."

She flicked his card with her thumb and dropped it into her bag. "Which pretty much puts me in the category of a threat, wouldn't you say?"

"Definitely," Steve admitted. What other way could he describe a woman who looked like heaven and lied like hell? "But I'm curious. If you're so confident about what you've got to offer, why did you risk it all for one look inside that house?''

"Because it's a ridiculous rule." Her smile faded and her gaze drifted out over the ruined garden. "And I didn't have much to lose anyway."

"Why would you say that?"

She waved a hand as though clearing a fog. "Never mind. Now if you'll excuse me, it's getting late."

He told himself to let her go, that he didn't need to know more. And found himself taking a step toward her instead. "Eden, tell me."

Those eyes were on him again, as sharp and clear as ever. He could see her measuring, deciding whether or not to speak. Then she dropped her bag and squared her shoulders, and it occurred to Steve that he should have let her go when he had the chance.

"Okay," she said. "But let me ask you something first." She moved toward him, her steps slow and deliberate. "Are you married?"

It was Steve's turn to step back. "Not that it's any of your business, but no, not anymore."

"I'm not surprised." She flashed him that sunshine smile. "Nothing personal. It just seems that everyone I know is either divorced or thinking about it. Kind of shoots holes in the idea of 'happily ever after,' doesn't it."

"That's a pretty pessimistic outlook."

"Or realistic, depending on your point of view." She tilted her head to the side. "And I assume yours is still optimistic?"

It was, but he saw no reason to get into it with her. "Eden, where are we going with this?"

"With any luck, straight into this house." She smiled prettily, too prettily, as she edged closer. "The reason I was willing to risk my spot as a finalist is because I know for a fact that the Board is going to put a family into that house.''

''Who told you this?''

''That's not important. What matters is that the neighbors on Devon have been quietly putting pressure on the Board ever since the contest was announced. They've lived with Rusk's mess for so long, they figure they have the right to demand a little stability now.''

''And that automatically means a family?''

''On Devon Avenue it does. And since the Board gets a lot of financial support from this end of town, they're not about to rock the boat.'' She glanced around, then lowered her voice and leaned in close. ''Well, we can be that family, Steve. You and me.''

He stared into those wide, gray eyes. ''You want me to marry you?''

''Not a chance,'' she said, laughing. ''But I do want you to pretend. The way I see it, with your background and my video, we can't miss.''

He tapped his pockets, suddenly needing a cigarette. ''You're suggesting we go into the interview as a married couple?''

She hesitated a moment. ''No, you're right, that won't work. Marriage is too complicated. But engaged is perfect. With a wedding coming up very soon.'' She snatched up her bag and took hold of his arm, leading him out to the street. ''Picture it. A September wedding in the garden. Under the gazebo. Should be beautiful that time of year.'' She screwed up her nose. ''How long do roses bloom anyway?''

Steve felt his head starting to spin with an image of Eden in a tangled wedding gown at the center. He drew up short, refusing to be led any farther. ''This is ridiculous.''

She shrugged in that offhand way of hers. ''Okay, a

church then. Either way, the board will love it. Now, the breakup will have to be carefully planned. Just small signs of trouble at first, then a very public fight and wham, 'happily ever after' is over.'' She nodded, obviously pleased with her scenario. ''Works for me.''

''Well, it doesn't work for me.''

Her expression turned so reasonable, he was sure he'd gotten through. ''You're worried about the division of property, aren't you? Well, we can settle that right now. Do you want the house?''

''Why else would I be here?''

''Any number of reasons, but the important thing is that I don't. Which makes it easy, agreed?''

He was still working on the fact that she didn't really want the house as she continued.

''So you give me the restoration money, I sign over the house and I'm gone before you know it.''

He shook his head, needing to slow things down, to call a stop there and then. ''Eden, it's no good.''

She smiled sympathetically. ''You need the money, too, huh? Okay, half will keep me going for a year anyway, and you pay me the rest after that. It's very straightforward.''

He dropped his head back, drawing in a deep breath and cursing himself for having left his cigarettes in the truck. ''How can you even suggest this? We don't know anything about each other.''

''How much do we need for an hour interview?'' She waved a hand. ''Oh, all right. I hold a degree in English and one in film and video. I have an editing suite I love, a camera I tolerate and Michael.''

All that stayed with him was the name. ''Michael?''

''We work together. Or at least we used to until he asked me to marry him. Which is why I need this house.'' She grinned at him. ''See how simple it is?''

Steve strongly doubted that anything about Eden Wells could ever be simple. "Look, even if I thought it would work, which I don't, what would we tell the judges?"

"A chance meeting, a whirlwind romance, happens every day. And when we split up, everyone will just think it's natural. Trust me, it's perfect."

Trust her? Hardly. "Eden, I have friends here. People who know I'm not engaged."

"So you've been keeping me a secret." She eyed him suspiciously. "Are you always so unimaginative?"

"Sometimes I'm very imaginative." Without pausing to think, he ran his fingertips along her jaw to her tender nape, enjoying the way her breathing faltered when he pulled her closer.

"Then prove it," she whispered, swaying against him.

He wanted to. Wanted to feel that lithe body pressed hard against him once more and discover what those lips could do when they weren't in motion all the time. He cupped her face in his hands, feeling her soften to his touch.

He bent to her slowly, liking the way she held his gaze, her eyes never wavering, the invitation clear. Was it real, or just another ploy? With Eden, who could tell? And he had no time to find out.

He set her back on her heels. "Sorry, Eden. But I never work with partners."

3

The sun sat high in the sky, the scent of roasting sausage was everywhere and Kilbride was in a party mood. Up and down Wickham Street, racks of bright summer clothes fluttered on the sidewalks, umbrella tables and plastic chairs transformed the smallest squares of concrete into outdoor cafés, and Saturday traffic had given way to makeshift stages where mimes, jugglers and clowns entertained. But all of it was lost on Eden.

She sat on the stone wall outside the library, a tub of warm, sweet caramel corn cooling in her lap while she studied the *Dreams of Devon* sign by the stairs. The illustration was modeled after a child's drawing of a house, complete with blue sky, fried-egg sun and purple stick family. But the library itself was a somber affair of narrow windows and heavy brickwork. A building with absolutely no sense of humor, Eden mused. The perfect setting for the afternoon's solemn proceedings.

She felt her stomach slide as an image of dark eyes, as fathomless in imagination as they were in real life, flashed through her mind, reminding her what a fool she'd been. She still couldn't believe that she'd been ready to kiss him. Not only ready but weak-kneed and waiting, wanting nothing more than to feel his mouth on hers.

Eden gave her head a shake and looked away. She would

definitely have to think about that later, but right now she had to figure a way to get her hands on that house. She held out the popcorn container to the woman beside her. "Come on, Nicole, you must know someone who'd pose as my fiancé for fifty thousand dollars."

Nicole Boothe frowned as she sucked caramel from her fingers. "Look, if I thought it would work, I'd dress up as a man and go in with you myself."

Eden looked over at her and the line between Nicole's precision-plucked brows deepened. "I was kidding."

Eden laughed and shoved a hand into the popcorn. "Thank God."

Nicole might be her best friend and favorite bartender, but there was no way she was going to go into any interview with a five-foot-three-inch fiancé on her arm. Especially one with tiger stripes on his fingernails. "But seriously, with all the men you meet at that pub, you have to know at least one who'd do this."

"The only man worth knowing in that pub is mine. Or at least he will be one of these days, so forget it."

Deiter, Eden remembered. New owner of the pub, recently divorced and extremely gun-shy. Eden shook her head. Nicole always had loved a challenge. Eden tossed a few kernels into her mouth. "I don't want to keep him. Just borrow him for a few hours."

Nicole let her breath out in a huff, helped herself to another handful of caramel corn and slid off the wall. "Let it go, Eden."

"How can I?" She rose and followed Nicole into the crowd. "You're the one who told me the Board wants a family in that house."

"And I wish I'd kept my mouth shut." Nicole chewed furiously as she picked up the pace. "It's only a contest, for God's sake. Another long shot. If you win, great. If you lose, you go home and pick up where you left off.''

Eden almost laughed. "And how will I do that? Waltz into Michael's office and tell him I'd like my job back? Explain that while I still won't marry him, I've decided we can work together after all?'' She shook her head, recalling Michael's face when she'd handed back the ring. The one everyone at the office knew was hidden inside her camera case. Everyone except Eden. She winced and stuffed more popcorn into her mouth. "Knowing Michael, he'd have me thrown out before I even reached his office."

"The man always was an idiot," Nicole muttered. "So who needs him anyway? It's time Footloose was up and running anyway. God knows you've spent enough on equipment.''

"Which is why I won't last a month without some kind of steady work." She sighed and handed the popcorn to Nicole, her appetite suddenly gone. "Without the money from that house, I'll be right back where I started, doing weddings and bar mitzvahs just to survive. And the only ones who'll know how close I came to getting out are you, me and Steve Cooper.''

As though speaking his name had summoned him, Eden turned and spotted him across the road at a café. "Like a bad penny," she murmured and moved a little to the left for a better view. He was leaning back in the chair, smoking a cigarette and laughing at something one of the men at the table had said.

Clean-shaven now, his hair combed back from his face, Eden had to admit he looked even better than before. For a cowboy. She nudged Nicole. "That's him. The one in the denim shirt.''

Nicole made a low, approving sound deep in her throat.

"Why is it that the guy you want most to hate is always the best of the bunch?"

Eden gave her best casual shrug. "He's okay, I guess. If you like the type."

"Since when have you changed?"

"Since I discovered therapy."

Nicole only laughed but Eden was adamant. "It's true," she insisted. "There's just no way to read a man like that, no way to know what he's thinking. He sits there looking so laid-back and comfortable you'd swear the whole world is passing him by. Then too late you discover he hasn't missed a thing." She took an unconscious step closer. "Makes me want to walk over there and twist his nose, just to let him know he's not fooling anyone."

"So do it. At the very least it'll make you feel better."

Eden considered it for a moment, then shook her head. Calling his bluff would probably be a little like waving a bandanna in a longhorn's path. And she wasn't sure she could run that fast. "I think I'll just leave well enough alone."

Nicole blinked. "That's a first."

"Which proves my point. A man like Steve can ruin a woman completely." Eden linked an arm through Nicole's and ducked back into the crowd. "Now, about the pub…"

Steve dropped some bills onto the waiter's tray, picked up his beer and walked to the edge of the patio. Even in a crowd, she was easy to follow.

The oversize sweatshirt had been replaced by a light summer dress that left her shoulders bare but was disappointingly long, covering her legs completely. That sungold hair had been caught into a ponytail on top of her head, and Steve found himself smiling as he watched it bob up and down every time she laughed.

Her friend disappeared into a pub but Eden lingered at the lottery booth, running her finger over the glass, pointing out the tickets she wanted. When she nodded and reached into her bag, Steve wondered idly if she was still carrying her crowbar, but all she produced was a wallet.

She scratched off the seal, frowned, and dropped the ticket into a bin as she headed off. Steve took a few more sips of his beer, set the bottle on the table and made his way to the gate—telling his friends he had something to do. Telling himself it was simply time to go.

She was at the library by the time he caught up with her, reading the poster that welcomed the *Dreams of Devon* finalists and showed a picture of the house as it had been nearly one hundred years ago.

"Lining up your next window?" Steve asked as he drew up behind her.

A flicker of surprise, a moment of panic, then she went back to studying the picture. "Why not? I still don't have much to lose. Unless of course, you've changed your mind."

He stood close enough to discover the subtle scent that surrounded her. Vanilla and something else. He closed his eyes and inhaled deeply, quietly. Musk? Vanilla and musk. Like ice cream and sex. An interesting combination. Almost enough to make a man forget what was important. He took a step back. "Like I said, I don't work with partners."

"Then my idea makes even more sense." She twisted around to look at him. "Just say yes and before you know it, you won't even have a partner anymore. I'll go back to New York and you'll walk away with that house free and clear."

"And you, Eden. What do you walk away with?"

She shrugged and turned back to the poster. "The money, of course."

"That's not all, is it?"

"What else could there be?"

"That's what I'm trying to figure out. You're pushing so hard, there has to be more." He put a finger under her chin, gently bringing her back. "What are you really getting?"

Her smile was a sad, crooked little thing. "A chance," she said so softly he wasn't sure he'd heard correctly. "So I don't have to sell kiwis anymore."

Steve had always been known for his clearheaded decisions. But if he looked into her eyes any longer, he knew this time might be the exception. And he couldn't afford to be wrong.

He released her. "Sorry, Eden, but I can't."

She swung the bag up onto her shoulder and scanned the crowd. "Then I'll just have to find someone who can."

"You're not serious."

She glanced back at him. His tone was light, casual, but his eyes told her something else. What was it she saw behind those thick black lashes? Anger? No, not nearly dark enough. Concern then? That was it, she realized and almost smiled. So the immovable Steve Cooper was finally concerned about losing the house. Now they were getting somewhere.

"I'm very serious," she said and made a sweeping gesture at the crowd. "Take a look around. Do you honestly think I'd have trouble finding a man who'd do this for, say, twenty-five thousand dollars?"

"You want me to believe you'd walk out there and just ask some stranger to go into the interview with you?"

She smiled at him. "I asked you, didn't I?" She narrowed her eyes and pointed to a guy who obviously spent too much time at the gym. "And I think I've just found bachelor number two."

She was halfway down the stairs when Steve caught up to her. "I can't let you do this."

She glanced up at him. "Are you saying you'll come in with me?"

"Not a chance."

The man was impossible. "Then you'd better step aside," Eden said. She started to pull away when a little boy raced by, all blond curls and baseball glove, nearly colliding with her on his way to the door. A slender woman in a prim lavender suit was only steps behind. "Tanner Binnington," she called. "Do you want Mommy to get mad?"

Eden snapped around. Binnington?

The woman raised a hand and pointed a finger at the little boy. "All right, Tanner, I'm getting mad," she said, and the child disappeared into the library.

While the woman continued up the stairs, Eden pulled Steve to the side. "That's them," she whispered. "The Binningtons of Boston. The other finalists. The family the board will give that house to unless we do something."

He shook his head. "Eden, I still don't buy it."

"Then maybe the weight lifter will." Eden turned, searching for the perfect pecs but catching sight of the poster at the bottom of the stairs. The stick family smiled back at her, their purple faces not unlike the color of Mrs. Binnington's suit. Coincidence? Not likely.

She looked back to see Tanner's mother waving to a man and woman at the bottom of the stairs. "John, honey, the little monkey's gone again. You and Helen bring the kids. I'll meet you inside."

Her husband adjusted the sleeping baby in the pack on his chest while Helen, a slightly older version of Mrs. Binnington, lifted a toddler into her arms and trudged up the stairs behind him.

Helen glanced at Eden as the child's sticky fingers reached out and grabbed her skirt on the way by. "That's just apple juice," she explained as she opened the door. "It'll wash right out."

Eden stared at the stain on her dress while the door closed behind the Binningtons. "I can see why they want a family so badly."

Steve took her hand and led her inside. "Come on. We'll get some water on that."

The library was cool, dark and quiet, smelling of floor polish and leather. From the balcony above came the sounds of running feet and a distant voice, calling "Tanner, don't you dare throw that ball."

Steve was still looking for a water fountain when Eden heard a door close behind them. She turned as two men and a woman stepped into the hall, each carrying a black portfolio and wearing a *Dreams of Devon* button, identifying them as judges.

"There's a fountain," Steve said and walked on, but Eden held back. Tanner flashed by in the hall behind the judges, baseball raised and ready for launch, with Mr. Binnington in pursuit this time.

"Sweet kid," Eden muttered as Mrs. Binnington and Helen appeared from out of nowhere, hands outstretched and smiles in place for the judges.

Eden was too far away to hear what was said, but close enough to see the female judge reach out to stroke the baby's pink cheek while the men smiled at the toddler. And bringing up the rear, Mr. Binnington with Tanner in one hand and the baseball in the other.

The judges spoke to the Binningtons like old buddies, laughing and chucking the children under the chin. Eden told herself to stay calm, to think. But all she could see was Tanner Binnington's baseball crashing through the stained-glass window of that house, shattering her dreams. And all because Steve Cooper refused to see reason.

Frustrated, she waved him over to where she stood. "Still don't buy it huh?" She pointed along the hall. "Well, take a look down there and tell me those judges haven't already decided who's moving into that house."

Steve sighed and took a look. A long look. Then he turned to see Eden staring at the front door. Getting ready to make a move on the weight lifter, or just biding time? And would she tell him the truth if he asked? Probably not. So he stepped in front of her, blocking the view. "What was the name of that film school you went to again?"

The hallway leading to the South Common Room was dimly lit and deathly quiet, the only sounds the ticking of the clock and the echo of their footsteps on the hardwood floor.

Eden checked the page in her hand. Steve was thirty-one, born in Nevada, raised on a ranch. She smiled and glanced over at him. She'd known all along there was a cowboy in there somewhere.

She tucked the page into her bag and focused on the interview. "Let's go over this one more time. The wedding will be small, and I don't have a ring yet because it's still being made." Eden stopped short and pulled the page out again. "What shape was the diamond again?"

"Teardrop." Steve shifted the folder he'd retrieved from the truck to his other hand. "Don't worry. And don't be so nervous."

She shoved the page into her bag. "I'm not nervous."

His fingers found the precise spot where her shoulders were already knotted. "Yes, you are."

She plucked his hand from her shoulder and let it drop.

"I'll be fine." She paused with her hand on the doorknob. "But are you sure you're ready?"

He laid a hand over hers and opened the door. "Watch and learn."

The judges sat at a long oak desk at the back of the room, their names scrawled on folded pieces of cardboard in front of them: Noel was cool and unruffled, Mark bald and weary and Joanne round and blond with fluttering fingers.

Steve set his folder on the table.

"I'm Steve Cooper and this is Eden Wells." He flashed that wonderful grin. "How are you folks today?"

Joanne hesitated a moment, then smiled. "A little surprised." She took the hand Steve offered. "It's a pleasure to meet you, Mr. Cooper, Miss Wells."

There was something to be said for downhome charm after all, Eden thought, relaxing just a little as she laid her proposal beside his.

"I believe this is Miss Wells's time slot," Noel said.

Eden opened her mouth but Steve was already there, taking the lead, his voice smooth and relaxed as always. "I'm sure my being here comes as a shock to all of you. I know it did for me. But the reason is simple." He reached for her naturally, casually, his arm circling her waist as though it really was his right. And she found herself moving to him, with him, as though her place was there beside him. "You see, Eden and I are engaged to be married."

Noel's mouth fell open. "Married?"

"In the garden," Eden offered. But her mind wasn't on the house or the wedding. She was too busy thinking about the faint but unmistakable warmth pooling deep inside as Steve's fingertips brushed her hip, coaxing her closer still.

"Let me explain," Steve said.

She looked up at him wondering how a touch could seem so casual, yet feel so intimate at the same time.

"You see, Eden and I met a while ago at the house on Devon. We were both there one morning having a look and discovered we were both finalists. We got to talking, one thing led to another and the next thing we knew, we were discussing a wedding and happily ever after. Isn't that right honey?"

"Hmm?"

One brow raised and Eden realized she was staring. "Oh, yes," she said, quickly checking herself and shifting her attention to the judges. "Happily ever after."

Noel's gaze flicked from Eden to Steve. "You didn't know each other before the contest, yet now you're getting married?"

"A real whirlwind," Eden told him at the same time Steve answered, "Just a chance meeting."

"What a happy coincidence," Joanne said.

"That's it exactly," Steve agreed. "A happy coincidence."

"Why didn't you tell us before now?" Noel asked.

"To be honest," Steve said, "we were afraid you might not believe us, and that it might jeopardize our chances of winning. But we finally decided honesty was the best policy after all, so here we are. And if anyone has any concerns about our relationship, I'd like to address them now."

He looked from one judge to the other, as though they were the ones with something to explain. Eden held her breath.

Joanne shook her head. "I can't think of any reason to object."

"It does simplify things," Noel agreed and Mark dropped his head down on the desk. "Can we just get on with this?"

Steve smiled. "We're as anxious as you are."

Eden released her breath and looked over at him. The

man had a way of turning a situation around, that much was clear.

"But," Noel interjected, "since you're asking us to consider you as a couple now, you're only entitled to an hour." He held up a hand when Eden started to protest. "One finalist equals one hour. It wouldn't be fair to the Binningtons otherwise, would it?"

The bloody Binningtons again. Eden felt herself smiling too hard and consciously relaxed. "An hour will be fine."

Joanne pushed a pair of glasses onto her nose. "Now, what we're most concerned with today is finding the right person for the Rusk home."

Joanne reached for Eden's proposal, but Steve took a step forward and slid his folder across the table. "And I believe you'll find everything you're looking for right here." He glanced over at Eden. "Why don't you have a seat, honey? This could take a while."

Eden watched as her proposal was set aside and Steve's folder flipped open. This wasn't the way they'd planned it, but unless they wanted to start breakup rumors right now, she didn't see that she had much choice.

So she forced a smile and sat, letting Steve take the lead. His recommendations were probably the more natural starting point anyway, she told herself. And her proposal would make the perfect close.

"Saw the work you did on the Buckman house a few years back," Noel said as he turned a page. "Very impressive."

"I was pleased," Steve said and sent Eden a quick, cocky grin.

"But I have to say," Mark continued, "that I disagreed with your choice of ceiling medallion in the dining room. Rococo was a bit of a stretch, don't you think?"

Eden smiled at Steve, wondering how deep the teeth marks on his tongue would be when he finally spoke.

"That house," he explained, his tone so patient it sent a chill down her spine, "had been renovated many times and lost most of the original flavor. But the traces I did find assured me that the medallion is absolutely correct."

"I suppose," Mark said, then tapped a finger on the page. "So what is this by the kitchen?"

"A conservatory," Steve said, his shoulder relaxing as he leaned over the drawing.

He fielded their questions and laughed easily, putting everyone at ease. Soon Mark was smiling, Noel was nodding and Joanne was caught up in the sketches. Even Eden found herself being pulled into his excitement, his vision.

He turned to the next drawing, and Eden could see Tanner's baseball suddenly veering off, missing the mark completely. All they needed to clinch the deal was one look at her presentation. She nudged her folder forward as a not so subtle reminder.

"We're not quite finished, honey," Steve said and slid it back. "Now if you'll take a look at the rose garden," he continued and Eden slumped back, thinking Steve and those rosebushes had a lot in common.

"In conclusion," Steve was saying. "I want you to know that the house on Devon has always been a personal favorite of mine." He smiled at Eden. "And I know Eden fell for it the first time she saw it. Didn't you, honey?"

"It was all because of you, dear." She gave him a tight smile, then turned to the judges. "But my proposal will show how strongly I feel about the house, and offer the Historical Board something unique at the same time."

"I'm sure it will," Noel cut in. "And I promise we'll have a look at it before we make our final decision, but I'm afraid your hour is up now."

She rose slowly. "All I need is a few minutes."

Noel packed up his notes. "I'm sure the Binningtons would have appreciated an extra few minutes, too."

She took a step toward the desk, but Steve wrapped an arm around her, pulling her back. "We understand," he said, and Eden could see that baseball turning around, heading straight for her.

Joanne smiled. "Then we'll see you at the house at five o'clock." She held up Eden's proposal. "And I'll be sure to have a good look at this."

Steve tightened his grip on Eden's waist while the judges filed past. "Don't say another word," he muttered. "Or you'll put us right out of the running."

She jerked away from him as soon as the judges were out of sight. "I was never in the running." She grabbed her bag and swung it over her shoulder. "Thanks to you."

"What are you talking about?"

"I'm talking about the way this interview turned into the Cooper Construction Hour."

"I only gave them what they wanted."

"I had something they wanted, too, Steve."

"Something you hoped they wanted. But when they limited us to an hour, I couldn't take that chance. I've waited too long for that house to risk my only shot on a whim."

He reached out to pick up his folder but Eden slapped a hand on it, holding it still. "This was my shot, too."

He lifted only his eyes. "I did what I thought was best. And I told you from the start that I don't work with partners."

"I'm not surprised." She shoved the folder toward him and headed for the door. "You don't even understand the concept."

4

By four-thirty, Devon Avenue was lined with cars, the mayor was posing for pictures and lemonade stands were springing up everywhere. On the porch of number sixteen, a podium sat in front of a long cloth-covered table, and on the lawn, a noisy crowd waited to find out who the winner would be.

Mr. Binnington and the children were nowhere to be seen, but Mrs. Binnington was standing beneath a huge oak tree, confidently chatting up the neighbors with Helen while her high heels slowly sank into the grass.

"Already taking root," Eden muttered as she climbed the stairs to the porch.

"Forget about her, and pretend you're glad to see me."

She wished she'd noticed Steve lounging on the railing earlier, but there was no way to change course now. So she crossed to the table and dropped her bag on the floor. "I'll be glad when this is over."

"So will I."

She watched him come toward her, arms loose at his sides, steps long and unhurried. Not a cocky strut by any means, but the walk of a man completely at home in his skin. He stopped in front of her, not quite touching, but near enough that she could feel the heat of his body on her bare skin. "But we're supposed to be the happy couple, remember?"

It wasn't her way to hold a grudge, but since it obviously wasn't his way to apologize, she figured he'd earned it. She dipped her chin and gave him a lovely smile. "I'll be happy if you leave me alone."

"It's a little late for that." He bent and touched his lips to hers. It wasn't even a kiss really. Just the kind of quick, friendly brush any couple might share. But it left Eden feeling restless and frustrated, anything but friendly.

She reached up and patted his cheek, consciously resisting the urge to slap it. "Not for much longer."

She turned at the sound of footsteps on the stairs. Mrs. Binnington winked at Eden as she stepped onto the porch, then mouthed, "Good luck," to them both before returning her attention to the judges coming up the stairs behind her.

Shrewd and aggressive, Eden conceded as Mrs. Binnington sat down beside Steve, but with a touch of class. There had to be a place for a woman like that, Eden acknowledged. And only hoped it wasn't on Devon.

The crowd quieted and shuffled closer to the porch as the mayor took his place at the podium. "Ladies and gentlemen, welcome to the *Dreams of Devon* finals."

Mrs. Binnington lowered her gaze to her hands, her expression so serene it bordered on beatific. It was such an obvious ploy. Such a pathetic attempt to garner favor. And Eden silently cursed herself for not having used it first.

Steve's hand was hard and cool, his grip firm as he pulled her hand into his lap. "Don't worry," he whispered and twined his fingers with hers.

Damn him, she thought. But couldn't bring herself to pull away.

"Over the years," the mayor continued, "the Rusk House has often annoyed, sometimes frustrated and frequently embarrassed. But it has never failed to fascinate, which is why this contest makes such a fitting conclusion to the Rusk legacy. So without further ado.'' He turned to the finalists and held up a white envelope. ''Our winner.''

Mrs. Binnington moistened her lips.

Eden tried not to chew hers.

The mayor read the card then raised his head and looked around, his pause so well rehearsed it deserved a drumroll. ''Ladies and gentlemen, help me in welcoming Devon's newest neighbors, the soon-to-be-wed Steve Cooper and Eden Wells.''

Eden stared at the card as a reporter and photographer moved up the stairs.

''Miss Wells, over here please...''

''Mr. Cooper, look this way...''

Steve helped her to her feet. ''No more kiwis,'' he whispered, then his hand slipped away, leaving her oddly disoriented, lost in a sea of smiling faces.

She turned to find Joanne bearing down on her, her eyes misty as she shook Eden's hand. ''A fairy-tale wedding, right here in the old curmudgeon's house. It couldn't be more perfect. I wish you and Steve nothing but happiness.''

Eden smiled ruefully. Oh, they'd be happy all right. Just not together. Yet she didn't stop to wonder when she recognized the touch on her shoulders, the warmth at her back. Without conscious thought, she moved to him, and hands that were sure and strong responded, drawing her closer until she rested fully against his chest.

Steve's voice tickled inside her ear. ''That move was so good, it was almost enough to fool me, too.''

She stiffened and pulled away. ''Thanks. I appreciate a good review now and then.''

The mayor grinned as he came toward them. ''I'm sure the only thing on your minds right now is getting inside that house." He opened a small black box, revealing two gold keys. "Steve and Eden, welcome home."

Steve accepted the keys and the reporter elbowed her way in. "Mr. Cooper, your upcoming wedding has been dubbed the true Dream of Devon by folks here in Kilbride. Perhaps you could tell us why you kept your relationship a secret until today?"

"We'd be pleased to talk about it later," Steve said, taking Eden with him as he walked to the door. "But right now, I've got a beautiful woman to carry across the threshold."

While Steve unlocked the door, the reporter cornered Eden instead. "Miss Wells, perhaps you could give a few specifics. How you met, what kind of wedding you're planning."

"She's a little busy right now." Steve cut in, receiving a roar of approval from the crowded porch as he lifted Eden into his arms.

She smiled for the camera, recognizing a great shot when she was in it, then buried her face in his neck. "What are you doing?"

"Giving her something to report on." He kicked the door open, set Eden inside the house then turned her around to face him.

"Wasn't that enough?" she asked.

His arms circled her waist. "Not even close."

Eden was dimly aware of the camera as Steve flattened his palms against her back, drawing her nearer by degrees. "We're only acting, remember?"

His voice turned soft, husky. "And they're going to get a great performance."

She laid a hand on his chest, meaning to push him away. He only smiled. "Are you going to disappoint them?"

A tiny shiver ran through her and the stillness in his

hands told her he'd felt it, too. His gaze shifted, locking on her mouth.

She floated for a moment, then grabbed a fistful of his shirt and pulled him to her, wanting only to taste what she saw so clearly in his eyes, and ignore the fact that none of it was real.

He bent to her the way he had on the porch earlier, but there was nothing light or casual this time. Only the heat of his mouth on hers, and a soft, low moan from deep in his throat when she opened her lips, melting any resistance she may have had left.

He lifted his head and she wrapped her arms around his neck, her fingers threading through his hair as he walked her back a few steps. She heard in the distance the click of a lock and a burst of applause, and then nothing at all but his breath in her ear. "I think they bought it, don't you?"

The words drifted inside her head, taking their own sweet time coming together. But as he pulled away, she understood.

"Sure," she managed to say and forced herself to move, to think. What else had she expected? Sex on the stairs? Up against the wall, perhaps? They were acting, for God's sake. Playing a part, keeping up appearances. He didn't want her any more than she wanted him. They were each just a means to an end, a perfect arrangement. And the sooner she was out of there, the better.

She turned away and he made no move to stop her, so she kept going, putting one foot in front of the other, not caring where she was heading, only knowing it was safer to keep moving, to stay out of reach, at least until she could figure out what was going on.

She hit a switch at the end of the hall and the chandelier above her flicked on. Half the bulbs weren't working and the teardrops were coated with a layer of dust, but it cast enough light to bring the house to life, to make it real for the first time.

Tall narrow doors with crystal knobs and huge keyholes lined the hall, each one tightly closed. And on the newel post, a scowling brass dragon rose up, barring the way, making it clear she didn't belong.

The doorbell sounded above her, making her jump.

She spun around as the mayor poked his head through the door. "Sorry to interrupt, but the lawyer for the estate is here."

A tall man with a pinched expression stepped into the hall. "Nigel Goodman," he said, frowning as he took a quick look around. "Perhaps we should sign the papers outside." He motioned the mayor to follow. "We'll need a witness."

Steve sent her one of those easy smiles as they settled around the table on the porch and the mayor jumped right in. "You must be anxious to get this over with so you can get on with your plans."

Eden sat forward as Nigel passed out the contracts. "You have no idea."

"The deed is self-explanatory," Nigel explained. "As is the trust."

Eden looked up. "Trust?"

He clicked a gold pen and handed it to her. "Mrs. Elson has it all arranged. You take your proposals to the Board and they advance the funds. Provided they approve, of course. It's all explained on page three." He tapped a finger on the paper. "Sign here and here."

Eden shook her head, confused. "Are you saying we don't have direct access to the money?"

Nigel looked at her for the first time. "Did you really expect her to simply hand you one hundred thousand dollars and hope the restoration went well?"

Steve shifted beside her. "What else would we assume? There was nothing in the entry about a trust."

"It's a recent development," Nigel said. "On my recommendation in fact. And the entry clearly states—"

Eden held up a hand. "I know, I know, it's her contest. Was that your recommendation, too?"

Nigel folded his hands and smiled indulgently. "Miss Wells, you're free to arrange your own financing—"

"No," Steve said. "The trust will be fine."

"For you, maybe," Eden snapped and the mayor's eyebrows rose.

Steve sent her a quick, censoring look before turning back to the lawyer. "We'll take the trust."

Eden was about to protest when she caught sight of Mrs. Binnington and Helen with the reporter, all of them hovering at the bottom of the stairs, watching her closely. So she smiled and sat back, thinking that Steve and Mrs. Elson would get along just fine.

"It's only a precaution," the mayor said in tones meant to be consoling. "To be sure the restoration is handled properly. And with Steve's experience and your help, there shouldn't be any complications at all."

No complications? Eden almost laughed until Steve nudged the contract closer and whispered, "Just sign."

She glanced over at him. Of course he wanted her to sign. What difference did it make to him? Even with the trust, he'd still have half the house. A house he knew damn well she wanted no part of.

She dropped the pen and pushed away from the table. "I'm not signing anything until I speak to Mrs. Elson."

Helen and Mrs. Binnington were listening intently now, their eyes darting from Eden to Steve.

"Mrs. Elson's on safari," Nigel said. "But she's planning to visit Kilbride in about six weeks to see how things are coming along. You can speak to her then." He held out a hand. "In the meantime, I'll take the keys."

Steve put a hand over his shirt pocket as he got to his feet. "Give us a moment." He turned to Eden, but there was nothing easy about the smile he gave her this time. "Honey, can I have word with you?"

"Let me guess," she muttered as he led her back into the house. "You're about to make another decision for us."

"Someone has to." He closed the door firmly behind them. "What were you thinking about out there?"

"Myself, same as you."

He rubbed a hand roughly over his face. "I knew this was a mistake from the beginning."

"Funny, I'd assumed that since we are now standing inside the house we just won, that my plan was a success."

He turned on her. "Or maybe my drawings would have been enough on their own. While that's something we may never know for sure, I have no doubt that you are about to blow the whole thing for us now."

Eden let his remark about the drawings pass—for now. "All I want to do is talk to Mrs. Elson."

"And it's making people nervous. If Nigel takes this back to her, in six weeks we may find that she's done some investigating and we're out of the house altogether."

Eden folded her arms and frowned at the dragon on the newel post. "I don't see any other way."

Steve took hold of her shoulders and knew instantly it was a mistake. Her skin was too soft, her eyes too wide and her kiss too fresh in his mind, making him forget why they were there, and what he really needed from her. He pulled away slowly. "Look, I've waited a long time to get my hands on this house. Now that it's finally mine, do you think I'll just lie down and accept the trust, knowing every light switch, every chip of paint, will have to be approved by those three?''

She pursed her lips. "Poor baby. No rococo medallions."

He drew in his breath, forcing himself to relax, to go slowly. "Eden, I don't want the trust any more than you do. But if we play it right, Mrs. Elson's visit may be our ticket out."

She eyed him suspiciously. "How?"

Steve glanced at the door then drew her a little farther along the hall. "If we keep up the act for six weeks, convince the board and everyone else that the house is safe in our hands, then we may be able to persuade Mrs. Elson to drop the trust."

"And how will we do this?"

"We move into the house, keep a low profile—"

She held up a hand. "Stop right there. You expect me to move in here? With you?"

"Eden, we're supposed to be engaged. It would be perfectly natural for us to live here together. And it's a big house. You can take one floor and I'll take another. The only time we'll have to be together is in public."

She shook her head. "I don't know. What if it doesn't work? What if she still insists on the trust?"

"Then I learn to live with it and we carry on with the breakup."

"Which still leaves me with nothing."

Steve shook his head. "Look, most of my money is tied up in a house in Ohio. But once it's finished and sold, I'll make sure you get your half."

He pulled one of the keys from his pocket and held it out to her. "It's only for six weeks, Eden. What do you say?"

She hesitated and he held his breath, watching her play

out the scene in her mind. "I suppose it would look more natural if we were here," she said at last. "Living proof of the happy couple working together while they plan their fairy-tale wedding."

She reached out and closed her fingers around the key. "Okay it's a deal. Six weeks of domestic bliss outside and separate floors inside." She looked up him. "Partners then."

"Partners," he said, trying hard not to think of ice cream and sex as she swept past.

5

Steve stood in the doorway of the Honeymoon Suite, a duffel bag hanging from his shoulder and a cup of coffee between his hands. Inside the room, Jason McIsaac, an imposing man with a furrowed brow and a wealth of tattoos, looked over from the pillow he was trying to plump. "One word and you're dead."

Never one to ignore a threat, Steve set everything down and went to offer some help. But it didn't keep him from laughing. Jason was the finest friend and cabinetmaker Steve had ever known. But as the new owner of Wayside Bed-and-Breakfast, he had a lot to learn about the art of "fluff and puff."

"It's all in the wrist." Jason's wife, Anita, bustled through the door and set an armful of snowy white linens on the bed. Taking hold of the pillow, she flicked it once, set it in place, then rose up on her toes and pressed a quick kiss to her husband's lips. "Keep practicing. You'll get it."

She smiled and turned to Steve. "I thought you left days ago."

"Just picking up the last of my stuff," he said and kissed the cheek she offered.

She laughed, tossing Jason another pillow. "And how much of ours?"

Steve grinned and held up his hands. "Nothing this time, I swear."

In the week since he and Eden had signed the papers, Steve had begged a cot, some lamps, a few folding chairs and an old recliner from Jason and Anita, and moved himself into the house.

Camping out in a house he'd just bought was nothing new to Steve; he'd been doing it for years. Moving around the country, searching out old places in need of a little love and attention, fixing them up and selling them again was a way of life for him. The only difference was that this time, he'd be staying on.

"How's it been over there anyway?" Jason asked, his huge fingers plucking at a stubborn ruffle, trying to make it perk up.

Steve thought about the raccoons in the chimneys, the leak in the basement and the sagging roof. "Great," he said and walked back to where he'd left his coffee. "Although seeing this room finished is enough to make me think about coming back. It turned out beautifully."

Anita patted his arm as she passed. "You're welcome anytime. All you need is a bride." She snatched up his duffel bag and tossed it out the door. "A real one."

Steve glanced over as Jason approached. "Still not happy about this, is she."

Jason clapped him on the back. "She's coming around."

The duffel rolled along the carpet and bumped into the wall. A willowy blonde in bicycle shorts paused on her way up the stairs, watching as the bag came to a stop. Then she lifted her head and smiled at Anita. "Express checkout?"

Anita laughed and walked over to take her new arrival's bags. "Only for difficult guests."

The blonde's gaze flicked over Steve. "Are you really so difficult?"

He smiled. "Just misunderstood."

"How sad." She continued along the hall toward him. "Why don't you tell me all about it over breakfast?"

It was a good offer, better than most. And about a week too late. "Thanks, but I won't be around."

"Another time then. If *I'm* around." She drifted past him, flashed the kind of smile that told him she'd definitely be around if he wanted to find her and glided into her room.

Jason shook his head. "I never thought I'd see the day Steve Cooper would disappoint a blonde."

Steve set the cup down and bent to pick up his duffel. "Me, neither. Just make sure you keep her number handy after she checks out, because in six weeks I'll be a free man again."

Jason followed him down the stairs. "Do you really think it's going to work?"

Steve shrugged as he opened the front door and stepped outside. He'd wondered the same thing since the day they signed the papers. Going over it again and again, trying to come up with a different solution but always ending up in the same place—living in that house with a woman who didn't belong to him. One he would pretend to want in public but couldn't touch in private. Not if he was smart, anyway.

For all that she'd been tumbling in and out of his mind all week long, always turning up at the wrong time and disappearing again before he could make sense of it, Steve knew that Eden Wells was no more his type than he was hers. Had they met under different circumstances, they would have simply tipped their hats and carried on—he in search of a straightforward blonde, and her in search of God only knew what.

Even now, he had no idea where she was. She hadn't left a phone number or an address, or asked him for one, either. She'd simply slipped away, leaving him with nothing more than the list she'd given him before the interview, and realizing how little they knew about each other.

Yet if he closed his eyes, he could still hear the tremor in her breath as he touched his lips to hers, still feel her hands, so light on his chest at first, then suddenly stronger, pulling him closer as her mouth opened beneath his, and it felt as if he'd known her forever.

He tossed his bags into the back of the truck and forced himself to concentrate on what was real. "Of course it'll work." It had to. He glanced over at Jason. "You want to have a look at the layout for the kitchen?"

Jason smiled and opened the door. "Always."

Steve climbed into the truck and started the engine. "The way I figure it, if Eden and I just keep a low profile, the novelty will wear off and by the end of the month, no one will even remember our names."

Jason leaned an elbow out the window as they drove. "But there's been so much publicity."

"Only because it's still new. After a few more weeks with nothing to write about, the press will move on and we'll be known as that boring couple living in the old Rusk Place. It couldn't be more—"

He broke off as they turned the corner, his gaze moving past the Saturday morning gardeners and the Dumpster in his driveway to the blue cube van parked in front of his house. The back doors were open and a crowd was building around it, including his roofing crew, kids on bicycles and more neighbors than he had met all week. And smack in the middle of it all, long tanned legs and a smile that was all too familiar.

"What's she doing here?" Steve muttered as he pulled into the curb.

"She lives here?" Jason offered.

"Not for another two days." Steve shut off the engine and threw the door open. He glanced up at the house in time to see a man wrestling a huge godforsaken plant up the front stairs and through the door, where he passed a woman on her way out.

"And why is she letting all those people in the house?" Steve slammed the door and headed across the road. "The woman is going to blow this yet, I can feel it."

Jason jogged after him. "Remember the neighbors."

"How can I forget? She's got every one of them out there carrying her damn bags." He frowned as her shorts and crop top came clearly into view. "And why isn't she wearing more clothes?"

Someone pointed to him and waved, but Eden didn't notice. She was too busy laughing, smiling, playing to the crowd. Especially the roofer, he noted, and unconsciously picked up the pace.

"We hear you're a filmmaker," the roofer was saying as Steve reached the sidewalk.

Eden nodded and reached back into the van. "But not the Hollywood kind. My specialty is video." She held out a case to him. "Be careful with that, it's my camcorder."

A little girl dropped her bike on the grass and ventured closer. "Can I see it?"

"Why not?" Eden set the case on the ground and unzipped it. "In fact, this is probably a good time to get started on my latest video, 'Faces of Kilbride.'"

She glanced up at the house and slipped a small cassette into the camera. "How about a group shot on the porch for openers?"

Jason grinned and clapped Steve on the shoulder. "Somehow, I don't think boring is quite the word people will be using when they talk about you two. Now if you'll excuse me, I'm starting to see my name in lights,'' he added and trotted off to join the parade.

The roofer glanced up as Steve stepped onto the sidewalk. "Steve," he said, his voice no more than a startled chirp. "Good to see you. We were just going back to work."

Steve watched Eden's head snap up, saw her fingers still on the lens cap so briefly he was sure no one else had noticed. Then as the roofing crew slunk away, she put the camera down and sauntered toward him. "Steve. Honey." The scent of her perfume reached his head the same moment she planted a kiss on his cheek. "For the neighbors," she whispered, then turned back to the camera, dismissing him.

Annoyed that he had been left standing in her dust already, Steve grabbed hold of her belt and hauled her back. "No," he said, enjoying the startled look on her face as he wrapped one arm around her neck and settled her head in the crook of his elbow. "This is for the neighbors."

He didn't give her time to argue, simply covered her mouth with his, needing to set the pace, to make everything clear from the start. But her mouth was warm and soft and slowly opening—and it was only the sound of a Boston accent that made him lift his head.

"Well, here they are, Devon's own lovebirds." The woman bearing down on them was familiar. "I'm Helen Cormier, your next-door neighbor." She held out a hand. "You might remember me from the finals. Sylvie Binnington's sister?"

Eden's eyes were round and dazed, her footing unsteady, and Steve held on longer than necessary, wondering how much was real and how much was for the audience.

"Sylvie Binnington's sister is our neighbor," she said at last and pulled away to take Helen's hand. "Imagine that."

"I just got back from Boston," Helen continued, "and couldn't believe my luck at seeing you both out here. I'm planning a little get-together to welcome you to the neighborhood. Nothing fancy, just burgers on the barby, that sort of thing. How's tomorrow night?"

Eden smiled. "This is very nice of you, Helen—"

"But it's out of the question," Steve said, cutting her off before she could do any damage. "We'll be too busy with the house, won't we dear?"

She turned slowly and flashed him a brilliant, false smile. "He's right of course," she said, then shifted back to Helen. "But next Saturday will be fine. What can I bring?"

Steve stared at her, not quite believing what he'd heard. How much clearer could he have made it?

"Nothing," Helen said. "We just want a chance to get to know you better. And to hear all about this fairy-tale wedding of course."

Eden shrugged and eased out of her hold. "There's not much to tell."

"My dear, you can't leave these things much longer." Helen dipped her head and studied Eden closely. "Unless of course, you're not getting married in September after all."

Eden didn't miss a beat. "Oh, we are—in fact we were just talking about invitations the other day." She glanced up at him. "And I believe Steve saw one he liked, didn't you, darling?"

"But I'll leave it all up to you now, honey." It was his turn to smile as he leaned back against the van. She'd climbed out on that limb by herself; let her find her own way back.

Eden slanted him a look that told him she didn't need his help anyway, then turned to Helen. "Isn't that just like a man? Always leaving the details to someone else."

Helen opened her mouth to reply when a long, mournful wail from inside the van drew her attention. "Oh my, what a lovely cat."

Steve snapped his head around. "Cat?"

Helen glanced up. "You weren't expecting a cat?"

Eden pushed in front and pulled the carrier forward. "He was hoping I'd leave him behind."

"Can you blame me?" he asked as the cat let out another painful cry.

Eden scowled. "Don't be nasty," she said, then leaned close to Helen and spoke in a low, conspiratorial whisper. "Rocky's a sore point."

Rocky? Steve bent down and peered into the carrier. Somehow, long golden fur and sullen blue eyes weren't quite what he expected of a "Rocky." But then, this was Eden's cat, so it figured.

Eden picked up her camera and smiled at Helen. "I was just about to start taping. Would you like to join the cast?"

Helen gave her a patronizing little smile. "I'm not much for cameras, but you go ahead and do whatever it is that you do. I'll just watch." She folded her arms across her chest and glanced over at the porch. "So I imagine your families are really excited about everything that's happened. Your mother must be especially thrilled. A daughter's wedding is always so special."

"Oh, yes." Eden raised her chin and hollered to the group on the porch. "I'm going to start at the top of the house and pan down. When I give the signal, I want lots of teeth, okay?"

The group nodded, but Helen wasn't finished yet. "And she must be curious about the house as well. Just chomping at the bit to get out here and see what you've won."

Eden flipped off the lens cap. "Actually, Helen, my mother is out of the country at the moment."

Steve straightened as Helen raised a brow. "Out of the country?"

Eden nodded and reached into the van for the tripod. "South America."

Helen took a step closer. "Is she working there?"

"Last I heard, she was doing time for inciting a riot. But they say she'll be out for Christmas. She usually is." Eden tucked the tripod under her arm and smiled. "You're sure you won't join us in the shot?"

Steve shook his head. She'd done it again—a slick, evasive answer, then moved on, leaving Helen to catch up and him to wonder how much was true.

"Quite sure," Helen said, but a definite note of triumph was in her voice. "But that settles it. You definitely need help with this wedding."

Eden started to protest when a voice from the porch hollered, "Are we making a movie or not?"

"I've kept you long enough," Helen said, then waved at the group on the porch and headed off. "Don't forget next Saturday."

"Wouldn't miss it," Eden said, but when Helen was safely on her own front lawn, she set the tripod down and turned an accusing eye on Steve. "You could have helped me out a little."

"And you could have told me you have a cat."

She walked around to the back of the van. "It's not the same at all."

"You're right, it's worse. What if I was allergic?"

She stopped and looked back at him. "Are you?"

"Fortunately, no."

"There you go then."

She rounded the back of the van and Steve ran a hand over his face as he followed. This was going to be a very long five weeks. "At least level with me about your mother. Is she really in prison?

Eden shrugged. "Probably. There's always one social injustice or another that needs a champion. And Mom always was fond of the grand gesture."

"But you're not sure," he inquired, and she shook her head. "Then why in God's name did you say that to Helen?"

Eden reached into the van again. "She was fishing, so I gave her something. And I didn't see any harm in making it interesting."

"No harm? Eden, we're supposed to be keeping a low profile here."

"Yes, I know." She jabbed a finger in the direction of the porch. "And if you'll take a look, you'll see your performance is not going unnoticed."

Steve turned and sent a quick wave to the group on the porch while she dragged a plastic pan and a bag out of the van and held them out to him. "Rocky will need this for a few days. Just until he gets used to the house, then I can let him out again."

Steve stared at the bag. "You have no idea how happy that makes me."

"Well, it's nice that something can." She picked up her camera then stopped abruptly and looked over at Helen's house, all pretence and guile suddenly gone. "Tell me honestly, Steve, are we in trouble here?"

"With Helen?" He shook his head. "Every gingerbread castle needs a wicked witch," he said, and was absurdly pleased when she smiled again. "We just have to be careful. Which means—"

She held up a hand, and headed for the porch. "I know, I know, a low profile." She hoisted her camera up onto her shoulder and called to the would-be stars on the stairs. "Okay, when I give the signal, everyone smile."

Steve shook his head as he watched her go. Helen wasn't the problem at all. The real trouble was heading up his front walk at that very moment.

6

Wh ile Eden arranged her front-porch scene, Steve hoisted the cat carrier and the litter pan, then threaded his way up the stairs to the door.

Jason glanced down at the carrier as he passed. "Nice cat."

Rocky wailed in response.

"Oh, he's perfect," Steve grunted. "Just what every construction site needs. That and a film crew to capture every glorious moment."

He set the carrier down in the kitchen and dumped the litter into the pan. That done, he reluctantly flipped up the locks on the carrier and stood back as Rocky stepped into his life.

Suspicious blue eyes blinked up at him, then turned toward the sounds of laughter drifting in from the porch. "What you hear," Steve explained, "is the making of 'Kilbride, The Movie' or 'Strange Faces' or whatever it is she's calling it now."

Rocky pretended not to hear. With a flick of his bushy tail, he sniffed his way around a corner and out of sight. Which only confirmed what Steve already knew: A cat could never take the place of a dog.

"Go ahead," Steve called after him. "Find a secret passage or something." With luck, he wouldn't see the furry intruder for weeks. As he turned, he noticed the plant at the far end of the kitchen. "What the hell is that?" he muttered, scowling as he moved closer. It bore a vague resemblance to the umbrella plants his mother used to keep, although he'd never seen one so huge. Or so unruly. Or so ugly.

He lifted a branch and let it fall. The thing probably ate small animals for lunch. A smile curved his lips and he glanced over his shoulder, wondering where the cat was. Wishful thinking, he knew, and turned back to the beast, shaking his head as he walked around it. As big and ugly as it was, with all the workmen coming and going in the next few weeks, it would never survive there.

Not that it mattered. Whether or not the beast lived long enough to make the trip back to New York was no concern of his. Traffic patterns in the kitchen, however, were entirely another matter.

Bending down, Steve wrapped his arms around the pot and fought his way up the stairs, battling flailing limbs and grasping leaves all the way, and finally putting the beast down in the room that would be Eden's. The windows were bright and there was plenty of room. He stood back. Well, there used to be plenty of room. And now it was her problem.

As he went downstairs, more laughter floated in through the front door, accompanied by voices this time. "You sure about this?" a man asked.

"We haven't done it in years," another countered.

And then her voice, unmistakable even in a crowd. "It's going to work beautifully. Trust me."

"Don't do it," Steve muttered and rounded the corner into the kitchen to search for his cigarettes.

There was a shuffling of feet on the porch, more laughter and then suddenly the sound of four-part harmony. A barbershop quartet, Steve realized. And it was indeed working beautifully. Which was more than he could say for himself. He kicked the block that held the kitchen door open and it swung closed, successfully shutting out the next act.

He stepped around her boxes, hoping his cigarettes hadn't found their way under one of them, and realized there wasn't a lot of furniture. Just two long desks, an office chair, a futon-for-one and boxes and bags of equipment: VCRs, televisions, keyboards, spotlights, and smack in the middle, a box marked Editing Suite—the one she loved, as he recalled.

He crouched down in front of the box. It was large. He lifted it onto the counter. Heavy, too. He ran a finger along the line of tape, wondering who had helped her with the move in New York. Had she packed her van alone, or had there been someone with her? Someone who was missing her now and hoping she'd come back. Someone like Michael perhaps, the one whose marriage proposal had sent her running to Connecticut with a crowbar.

He smiled and turned the box around. It seemed most women he met these days were only too willing to take that walk down the aisle. The one in Ohio had even gone so far as to sign him up for a course for his birthday: Ten Weeks to a Committed Relationship. She hadn't been amused when he'd dropped out in two.

And then there was Eden, on the run from commitment and in love with an editing suite. The one inside that box.

"I'll show you how it works later if you like."

He snapped around to see her standing in the doorway with the cat, both looking smug.

"No, thanks," he said and stepped away from the box. "I was just starting to take things upstairs. Trying to make some room here." He glanced back at the box and had the grace to smile. "And I was trying to figure out what it is you love about your editing suite."

She put the cat down and propped the kitchen door open. "That's simple. It gives me what every woman wants." She crossed to where he stood. "Power."

She stood directly in front of him, clearly assessing him, and Steve found it hard to keep his irritation focused in the face of such a bold challenge.

He moved closer until they were standing toe-to-toe and was charmed by the blush that warmed her cheeks. And chastened by the fact that she didn't back down. "And all these years I thought it was great sex."

"That, too," she agreed, and laid a hand on the box. "But with what I have in here, I can access a single clip in seconds, create backgrounds no one has seen before and put any face I like on a kiwi. Even yours." Then she turned her back and strolled over to where her bags and boxes covered the floor. "Sex can never give me that."

"Ah, but can an editing suite keep you warm at night?"

She laughed and sent him a quick grin. "Of course not. That's why I have eiderdown." She knelt and dragged one of her bags toward her. "And while we're on the subject, don't ever kiss me like that again."

He leaned a shoulder against the fridge. "How would you like me to kiss you?"

She gave him a tight smile. "I don't want you to kiss me at all. You don't see those couples out there all over each other. A little restraint is in order."

Restraint. He considered the word. And rejected it. "I don't believe in restraint. Especially in a marriage."

It wasn't hard to believe. Nothing about him suggested he would ever restrain himself in anything he felt or did. And without warning, she could feel his kiss all over again.

Bending over a bag, she unzipped it and thrust a hand

inside. "Well, we're not married or engaged. All we are is roommates. And I don't want to be kissed by my roommate."

"Whatever you say." He motioned to the front door. "Is there anything left in the truck?"

"Rocky was the last of it."

"You didn't bring much."

"I always travel light." She rummaged around inside the bag, pulled out two bowls and a box of cat food, and Steve wondered where a spoiled cat and a woebegone schefflera fit into traveling light.

She filled one of the bowls and carried the other to the sink. "Which one is cold?" she asked, motioning to the taps.

"Both. There's no hot water."

She stared in disbelief. "How am I supposed to take a shower without hot water?"

"No shower, either."

She cast a suspicious glance around. "What kind of place is this?"

"A very old one. But there's a tub and we can heat water on the stove. It's only until the new water heater is in."

She filled the bowl with water and set it on the floor with the food. "Any more surprises?"

He thought about masked bandits in the chimneys and mice in the traps and decided it could wait. "Nothing major. From what I've seen, it looks like Rusk was maintaining the place until about the fifties, which means most of the systems are workable but limited." He nodded at her equipment. "And you should be able to run most of that off the temporary hydro service."

"Good, because I want to finish the video before I leave. I hate loose ends." She crouched down and opened another bag. "Which is why I came in. I need another battery."

"Eden, we need to talk about how this is going to work."

She continued to rummage through the bag. "Domestic bliss outside, strictly business inside. Seems pretty basic to me."

His gaze skimmed over legs that were long and firm, shorts that were cut just right and a T-shirt with thin, slipping straps. He dragged his gaze away, knowing what he wanted was pretty basic, all right, and out of the question. But the house was another matter entirely.

He slid off the counter and walked toward her. "But what are you going to say if someone asks about the house? Wants to know how the work is going? You can't fake it forever."

Eden pulled her hand out of the bag. She should have stayed outside. Just taken her chances with the battery and gone exploring, keeping a nice safe distance between them.

Without a job, she'd had plenty of time to think in the last week—too much if she was honest—and had come to the conclusion that: 1. "Dorothy Elson" was really a code name for a subversive senior citizens group bent on destroying the lives of young women everywhere, and 2. Steve Cooper was a man she'd do well to avoid.

And after that kiss on the sidewalk, she was more convinced than ever.

Instead of the light, easy touch she'd had in mind, his kiss had been hard and possessive, and she'd found herself floating again in that place only Steve seemed able to take her. A place she couldn't figure out no matter how hard she tried, and until she did, she was determined never to go there again.

But after their run-in with Helen, she knew he was right. It was time to talk.

"Okay, the house." She glanced around as she got to

her feet. Small windows, a sink deep enough to drown in and a distance between the fridge and stove that was enough to make her feet hurt just looking at it. "This is obviously the kitchen."

"Heart of the home."

She wrinkled her nose as she strolled. "Too bad there's no pulse."

"By the time I'm finished, it will be racing."

"Pretty sure of yourself, aren't you."

A slow smile curved his lips. "About some things."

Refusing the bait, she continued to wander.

"Not a lot of comforts," she continued, pausing in front of the long sheet of plywood on legs. "But the table is a nice touch. I've always been fond of Early American Workbench myself."

He laughed then, that low easy rumble she liked too much, and so she kept moving, poking into cupboards and around corners, discovering beer and steaks in the fridge, and coffee and sugar in the pantry—the only signs of life.

She glanced back at him. "The place is a lot cleaner than I expected."

"Mrs. Elson's cleaning team has been busy. Nigel must have told her we were moving in, because they were here first thing Monday morning."

"The woman certainly thinks of everything," Eden muttered then looked around. "Where's George?"

"Who?"

"The plant, where is he?"

"I took it upstairs. Like I said, I was trying to figure out where things went when you came in."

She couldn't help but smile. "How thoughtful." She picked up one of her boxes. "Maybe you'd like to continue the tour up there."

He took the box from her, so she swung her lighting bag

over her shoulder instead and followed him to the stairs, consciously ignoring the dragon on the newel post.

She was on the second stair when Rocky darted past, taking the steps three and four at a time, narrowly missing Steve's feet in the race to the top.

"Damn cat," Steve hollered and dropped the suitcase on the landing.

"He likes to be first," Eden explained. "It's a guy thing."

His scowl deepened. "It'll be a dead cat thing if he does it again."

"I'll be sure and speak to him about it," Eden said as she came up the last few stairs. She stopped on the landing and glanced around. "Is this my floor?"

"It's our floor."

"Ours?" Eden asked and pushed past him to take a look for herself. "Is this another of those surprises?"

Plastic drop sheets hung halfway down the hall and the other flight of stairs was blocked off completely. She looked back at him. "What is going on up there?"

"Water, squirrels, you name it." He picked up her case and started along the hall. "Turned out that Rusk was living only on the main floor by the time he died, so he didn't much care what was happening in the rest of the house. Which means our choice of rooms is limited at the moment."

She stayed where she was. "How limited?"

"Unless you want something on the main floor, the two rooms up here are it." He stopped and looked back at her. "Are you coming or not?"

Eden nodded and started along the hall, taking in the somber wallpaper and narrow closed doors. Obviously things didn't get better as you went higher.

Steve put a hand on one of the crystal knobs. "I've

stripped the wallpaper and patched the plaster, but the rooms are still rough." He pushed open the door. "This one's yours."

Eden took a few steps onto the hardwood and looked around. The room was huge with a cavernous ceiling and George taking up most of one corner. Plaster cherubs and a scrap of old wallpaper taped to the door told her she was probably standing in what had once been a very fussy, very pink boudoir.

But a soft breeze drifted through the windows bringing the scent of lilacs from the garden, and Eden figured her editing suite could fit in for a while.

"Other than the fact that I have a clear view of Helen's yard, I like it," she announced, then reached out and pulled the scrap of wallpaper from the door. "I gather you're saving this as a reminder of Rusk's madness."

"What you have there is a classic William Morris design. I've got an expert tracking it down for me now."

Eden turned the sample up the other way and studied it more closely. "Why would you bother?"

He took the square from her and smoothed it between his hands. "Tradition. It's what the house is, what it was meant to be." He turned and tacked the scrap back on the door. "I don't expect you to understand."

"Which is why this deal is going to work out just perfectly," she said as she walked over to where George sat basking in the sunshine. "Since neither of us wants what the other will have, there won't be any difficulty splitting the assets." But she couldn't help glancing back at the sample, wondering if it looked any better from a distance.

"He seems pretty comfortable there," Steve said.

"George?" She lifted one of the sagging branches. "He's a survivor. He'll be all right."

"Can I ask why you brought it?"

"He worries when I'm gone." She smiled as Steve came toward her "And I had no one else to take care of him. Not many people understand a plant like George."

"And you? Do you understand—" he caught himself, realizing he was about to refer to a plant by name "—a plant like that?"

Her smile turned thoughtful as she ran her fingertips over the glossy leaves. "More than you know." She turned to face him. "So where's your room?"

He crossed to a door Eden had assumed was a closet and turned the knob. "Through there."

Eden stepped around him. "This is a bathroom."

Steve walked through and opened a door on the opposite wall. "And my room is on the other side."

"So not only do I not have my own floor, but I also have to share a bathroom with you?"

"There's not much choice."

"I haven't shared a bathroom since college," Eden muttered and stepped around him, giving the room a quick once-over. It was large with a pedestal sink, ornate brass mirror and deep claw-foot tub. There was, in her opinion, plenty of room for a shower.

"What about Michael?" Steve asked

Eden glanced back at him. "What about him?"

"Didn't you share a bathroom with him?"

Eden laughed, remembering Michael's repeated attempts to leave a toothbrush at her apartment. He'd spent a fortune in replacements before finally giving up. She walked a little farther into the bathroom. "The most Michael and I shared was an office."

"But you were going to marry him."

Eden shook her head. "That was his idea, not mine. I'd already told him I couldn't ever see myself getting married." She paused to examine a shelf by the sink. Razor, shaving cream, toothpaste, an ashtray and a paperback. She flipped it over to check the title. "You read sci-fi?"

"Sometimes. So I gather you don't want a family?"

She shrugged. "I can't see it happening. I like my independence too much." She set the book down and wandered over to the tub. "You've heard the expression, A Room of One's Own? Well I think more in terms of a Town House of One's Own."

She looked back at the tub and on a whim, kicked off her sneakers and climbed in. She sat down, stretched out to see if her toes could reach the taps, then gave it a nod. "This could be fun for a while." She closed her eyes and let her head fall back as she dipped lower into the tub. "Very Jean Harlow."

"All you need are bubbles and a feathered wrap."

"You obviously know Jean," Eden said, smiling as she opened her eyes. He was leaning against the door frame, his hands in his pockets and a smile on his lips. He looked lazy and relaxed, as though he had nothing at all on his mind but what he was looking at. Which just happened to be her. And the shiver running through her was sudden and hot.

"So what do you think?" he murmured.

"I still prefer showers," she said and scrambled out of the tub. Cold ones.

Keeping her head bowed, Eden moved past him to find Rocky stretched out on the floor, sharing George's sunshine. It hadn't taken either of them long to get comfortable, she mused, as questions of loyalty ran through her mind.

"And what about the cat?" Steve asked.

"What about him?"

"It's just that we'll be living in a construction site. I thought he might be better off in a kennel or a shelter—"

She turned on him, all softness gone from her voice, her face. "Stop right there. That cat is with me, understand? I'm all he's got and I will not leave him in some strange place, wondering if I'm ever going to come back." She gestured to her bags. "So if you've got a problem with him, I'll pack up and leave right now."

The fury in her eyes was so real, so artless, his first instinct was to reach out, to hold her, to let her know she didn't have to fight so hard. His second was to stay right where he was. He held up a hand. "Slow down, the cat can stay. I only thought it would be best—"

"And that's the problem, isn't it? You, always doing the thinking." She tried to move past him, but he took hold of her hand, not wanting to leave it this way.

"Eden," he said and watched her eyes widen, saw her gaze slip to their hands, and his heart pounded harder when she stayed.

He pressed their hands to his chest, so close she could feel the beat of his heart, the rise and fall of each breath. Eden barely heard him speak her name as she studied the two hands resting there, one dark, one light; one soft, one hard. Hands from completely different worlds, with nothing at all in common, yet somehow fitting perfectly, if only for a moment.

He stroked his thumb across her palm, the callused pad finding the soft, sensitive flesh at the base of her thumb and lingering there, circling slowly, so wonderfully, maddeningly slowly that everything around her faded away.

Her eyes fluttered closed and she floated, lost in sensation and dimly aware of the warning inside her head. The one reminding her that none of this was real. She pushed him away, went to the window and saw Helen looking back at her, making her feel like an intruder in her own home.

Her own home. The words sounded strange inside her

head. Strange and completely wrong. She spun around and found Steve still there, his gaze steady as always, holding her still and making her restless at the same time.

She felt a humming in her blood, a tiny shiver along her spine, and knew if he only asked she would go to him. So Eden picked up her camera and did what she did best, what she had always done. She ran.

7

Eden pressed her eye to the viewfinder and smiled. Only a few minutes into Happy Hour and already The Bearded Collie was noisy and crowded. The latest in cappuccino technology hissed and steamed in one corner, while ancient blenders churned out sweet, frothy drinks in the other. Imported beer crossed the bar as often as cheap draft and delicate pastries were running neck and neck with chicken wings for first place in the kitchen.

Ties and jackets lay draped over chair backs, backpacks and briefcases jostled each other under the tables and music was a blend of country, rock and jazz, depending upon who was pumping quarters into the jukebox. And above the dance floor, a digital sign reminded everyone about All Sumo Saturday and Poets And Playwrights on Tuesday.

The Collie was like a favorite uncle, a little neurotic but fun. And no one looked twice when Eden and her camera lay down on the floor by the ladies' room, which suited her just fine.

She held the camera steady and panned right, happy to be left alone with a scene in her mind and a shot in the viewfinder—two things that could always take her mind off her troubles.

Since leaving Steve in the house that morning, she'd

cruised the town, capturing everything from grocery stores to playgrounds on tape. Most of it was useless, she knew, but as long as she was filming, she wasn't thinking about dark eyes or strong hands or anything else. And that was enough for now.

She panned slowly, searching for details and subtleties, not really sure what she was looking for, but trusting her instincts to let her know when she'd found it.

Eden was just about to zoom in on a pair of tapping feet when a scuffed sneaker filled the viewfinder.

"What are you doing?" Nicole asked.

Eden stretched her neck to look up at her. "Keeping a low profile?"

"You?" Nicole laughed and crouched beside her. "Not a chance." She hollered to Deiter to fill in at the bar for her, then leaned over the camera, following the line of Eden's shot. "So, how did things go at the gingerbread castle?" She pointed a finger. "Do you want me to move that french fry before you shoot?"

"No, it adds character." Eden jammed a fist under the lens to steady the camera. "And things went so well, I'm beginning to think this wasn't such a great idea after all."

"Now she decides." Nicole sat down beside her and stretched out her legs. "Too bad you don't have an option."

Eden sat up slowly. "There's always an option."

Nicole arched a brow. "What about Mrs. Elson?"

Eden shrugged. "What about her? It's not like she's made a rule about our living there." Eden snapped the lens cap on and leaned her back against the wall. "I mean, what if Steve and I have decided to live separately because we're saving ourselves for the wedding night?" She looked over at Nicole. "Celibacy is very big right now."

Nicole laughed, but Eden ignored her, already picturing

herself at a press conference, smiling demurely, lashes lowered just so, the essence of innocent feminity. And trying hard to picture Steve looking unsure, bashful even—and frowning when the image refused to form.

Stubborn as usual, she thought, pushing him to one side as she pressed ahead with her own plan. "It could work."

Nicole rose and walked back to the bar. "Not anymore." Reaching under the bar, Nicole fished out a newspaper. "You obviously haven't seen this."

Eden got to her feet and plunked herself down in front of the paper. On the front page, dead center, was a shot of herself and Steve in the doorway of the house on Devon on the day of the contest, taken just before the door closed.

Nicole tapped a fingernail on the page. "That kiss is destined to be a classic. Like the soldier and his girl after World War II. And believe me, there's not a soul in town who isn't green, including me."

"Come on, Nicole, it was an act."

Nicole's expression turned wistful. "I know, but there's a part of me that would like to believe it's real."

"Well, don't. This arrangement is strictly business." Eden flipped the paper around so she could see more clearly and immediately knew she shouldn't have.

She looked lazy and comfortable there in his arms, her eyes half closed, her mouth lifted, waiting. Steve was holding her close, tilting her back, as though she was truly his, as though they belonged together. As though the last thought on his mind was saving himself. She shoved the picture aside. "There has got to be a way out of this."

Nicole set a frosted mug of draft in front of her. "Don't count on it. Besides, I've already lied to so many people about you and this wedding that I found myself looking seriously at pink organza and floppy hats the other day."

She shuddered and leaned across the bar. "Face it, girl, you're stuck."

"I am never stuck." Eden pulled the glass toward her. "All I need is an idea, and I'm free of him."

Nicole tilted her head to the side and studied her closely. "If I didn't know better, I'd say this guy is getting to you."

Eden lifted the glass to her lips. "Don't be ridiculous. And don't look at me like that. You're the one who wants the picket fence, Nicole, not me. As the great Philosopher Queen once said, 'I think, therefore I'm single.'"

"And alone." Nicole turned the picture around and leaned her elbows on the bar. "You know, it never occurred to me until lately that I might end up living the rest of my life alone, my nights measured in frozen low-fat dinners. I just took it for granted that someday I'd have the husband, the kids and the dog."

Nicole's expression took on the kind of soft, wistful quality that always made Eden want to retch. She snatched the paper away.

"Next thing you'll tell me is that you used to dress up as a bride at Halloween."

"That or a princess," Nicole admitted, then shrugged. "It's a Southern thing."

Eden nodded and flipped the paper around. "Well, where I lived, the princess always got mugged. So I stopped believing in fairy tales a long time ago, and I fill my own stocking, too. And when I wake up on Christmas morning, I am never disappointed."

"True," Nicole agreed. "But then you're never surprised, either."

The table by the dance floor signaled for another round and Nicole headed off with a pitcher.

Eden swung her camera bag over her shoulder as she got to her feet. "I don't need surprises," she called after her, then picked up the paper again and jammed it into her bag, muttering. "All I need is a way out of that house."

She was halfway to the front door when it opened. Eden stopped dead as Mark and Noel, two of the contest judges, stepped into The Bearded Collie. She swung around and nabbed Nicole's arm as she passed. "What are they doing here?"

Nicole glanced over at the door and waved. "They hold their meetings here." She turned back to Eden. "How do you think I knew so much about the contest?"

"I didn't think about it." Eden looked around quickly. "I can't face them now. Is there a back door?"

Nicole shook her head. "But if you hurry, you can probably get out the front while they're settling in."

Head down, Eden slunk to the door. She glanced back once, then put her shoulder to the door and nearly fell when it was yanked open from the other side.

"Eden, how are you?"

Joannne Guys, the judge who had promised to read her proposal at the interview, stood in the doorway, a black portfolio still in her hand. Eden took a step back. "Joanne, it's good to see you."

"Same here," Joanne said, her smile so genuine, so trusting, Eden couldn't help feeling a twinge of guilt when they shook hands. "I thought you'd be busy at the house."

"I was, I mean we were. But I wanted to get a head start on the Kilbride video."

Joanne nodded in sympathy. "A wedding, a new house and a video—it's just too much" She rose up on her toes and peered over Eden's shoulder. "Mark and Noel are here somewhere. Why don't you join us? Relax a few minutes."

"I can't," Eden said too quickly, then stopped, forcing herself to go slowly, be natural. "As much as I'd love to, Steve's expecting me back."

Joanne nodded. ''Helen said you two were working too hard.''

Eden kept her smile intact. ''Helen?''

Joanne shifted her portfolio to her other hand and linked an arm with Eden's, drawing her to one side. ''She told me everything.''

''Everything?''

She lowered her voice. ''About your mother.''

Eden winced, and for the first time a low profile started to sound like a good idea. ''Joanne, what I said about my mother—''

Joanne shushed her and cast a quick glance around. ''Don't worry, mum's the word, so to speak. This stays between you, me and Helen. But we're very concerned that this wedding is going to prove to be too much for you and Steve to handle alone. The way you described it to us at the interview, this is no small undertaking.''

Eden tried to laugh it off. ''We'll be fine.''

''Helen figured you'd say that, which is why we're not taking no for an answer.''

Eden consciously composed her face. ''We?''

''Helen and I.'' Joanne patted the portfolio, her eyes crinkling as her smile widened. ''The moment she told me what you're facing, I went right out and picked up a few things to get you started. I was going to drop them off later, but since you're here, you might as well have them now.''

Eden stared at the portfolio. ''You shouldn't have.''

''Eden, that's what small towns are all about, helping each other, being part of a community.'' She raised a hand and waved. ''There's Noel and Mark by the window,'' she continued and pulled Eden along. ''Come on, I'm sure Steve won't mind if you're a few minutes longer.''

Noel smiled as they approached the table. ''Well, if it isn't Kilbride's little filmmaker. What are you drinking?''

Eden bristled beneath her smile. "Beer, please. And it's a video."

Noel held up his bottle, signaling the waitress for another. "Call it what you like, fact is you've caused quite a stir. I wouldn't be surprised if folks come knocking on your door, looking to be part of it." He chuckled and shuffled over on the bench. "Including the mayor."

"I'm flattered," Eden said, thinking how pleased Steve would be when he found out.

"Well, they'll just have to wait," Joanne said, then shooed Eden into the bench beside Noel. "There'll be plenty of time for the movie after the wedding."

"Video," Eden murmured, watching another escape route disappear as Joanne dropped her bag on the floor and slid into the booth beside her.

On the other side of the table, Mark looked up and gave Eden a brief nod, then dropped a thick manila envelope on the table in front of Joanne. "We've got them dead to rights," he said, an unmistakeable note of triumph in his voice. "Clear-cut case of fraud."

Eden's stomach dropped. "Fraud?"

"A developer," Joanne explained, her tone hardening while she went through the wad of pages. "Two women from Los Angeles bought a lovely old estate on River Road last year. Wanted to put up five monster homes with tennis courts and indoor bowling lanes." She huffed and shuffled back on the seat. "I ask you, who needs indoor bowling?"

Inmates, Eden thought, and smiled weakly as the waitress plunked two bottles on the table.

Noel handed one to Eden. "We managed to hold them off for sixty days while we tried to sell it," he said. "Had plenty of interest but not a single offer. Naturally they tore it down, but it never sat right with us. So we decided to do a little investigating."

"Investigating," Eden repeated, her throat growing dry.

"Damn right," Mark said and Eden was sure he'd never been so animated. "Turns out the real estate agent we thought was working for us was also being paid by the developer. The inspection report he was handing prospective buyers grossly overestimated the repairs needed." He sat back, smiling at the stack of pages. "Took a while but we nailed them."

"How nice for you." Eden raised the beer to her lips. "What are you going to do now?"

"Prosecute, of course," Mark said. "They'll do five years on the fraud charge alone I'd say."

Eden choked and Joanne slapped her on the back. "Are you all right?"

"Perfectly," Eden gasped. "Isn't that a little harsh?"

Joanne sat back. "Those women misrepresented everything from the beginning. If you ask me, five years isn't harsh enough."

"Five years," Eden mused, wondering if there was a market for inmate infomercials. And how Steve would feel about carrying the tripod.

Joanne shook her head. "I don't know who they thought they were dealing with here."

"I can't imagine," Eden said, and downed the rest of her beer.

Joanne slid the report back into the envelope and smiled again. "Let's move on to something more pleasant, shall we?" Reaching into her portfolio, she pulled out a pile of bridal magazines and flyers, stacked them proudly in front of Eden and sat back smiling. "A little something to get that wedding started."

"This is very sweet," Eden said, but couldn't move. The magazines were thick and glossy, the covers done in soft pastels with smiling brides and satisfied-looking grooms peering out at her—the kinds of magazines she'd studiously avoided for years.

She wanted no part of the airbrushed dreams or the reworked vows. Marriage to Eden meant ties that bind, and a binding by its very nature was tight, restrictive, with no room to breathe.

Even Michael, for all that he'd wanted to bind her, had been smart enough to put a prenuptial agreement in with the ring—ten pages of legal ramblings, detailing the exact terms and conditions under which the marriage would be taken apart and the pieces distributed. No hard feelings, right? But if escape was inevitable, why bother in the first place?

Why not just keep it light, keep it easy and move on while the memories were still good?

Eden ran a finger over the soft-focus lace on the cover.

And what about love? Nothing more than a word that slid off the tongue too easily and too often. Love 'ya babe, let's do lunch.

She knew what it was to believe in love, to play the princess waiting to be rescued. And she knew what it was to finally wake up and climb down from that tower alone, rescuing herself when no one else came.

She knew from experience that nothing lasts forever. Not anger or hurt, not even hate. So why put her faith in something as weak and shifting as love?

But she knew Joanne was watching her, so she smiled and lifted a magazine from the top, flipping slowly through the pages and marveling at the number of cards that had been fitted inside: invitations, shoes, headpieces, silver, table linens, honeymoons. It made her sweat just thinking about it. So she closed the cover and turned to Joanne. "Thank you. And Helen, too, of course."

But Joanne wasn't finished yet. "There's more," she

said, all but wriggling in her seat as she reached into the portfolio again. "Helen pulled a few strings and came up with this." Eden took the white card Joanne held out to her. "Those are as rare as hen's teeth this time of year, and even harder to come by."

To Eden it looked like a business card, nothing more, and her face must have said as much because Joanne laughed and touched a fingertip to the top of the card. "What you have there is an appointment next week at Featherstone's, Kilbride's only wedding specialists. They don't usually take on anyone less than a year ahead of the big day. But they'll make an exception for you and Steve, because no one in town wants to see you stuck."

Eden stared at the card. "Stuck," she murmured. And sinking fast.

By the time she arrived at the house, the sun had set and a cool evening breeze was ruffling the oak leaves. The Dumpster was no longer empty, the roof was covered with tarps and metal scaffolding had grown up one side of the house, looking for all the world like prison bars in the moonlight.

"This is not an omen," she muttered, and pulled her van into the curb.

Yanking her camera bag out of the back, Eden headed up the walkway to the porch.

Steve lounging on the railing, however, was definitely an omen. She meant to keep going, to ignore him completely, but she couldn't resist. She paused at the door and looked over at him. "What are you doing?" She dropped her bag and marched across the porch. "And why is my cat tied to the post?"

Rocky blinked the sleep from his eyes and yawned.

Steve glanced down at the cat. "I didn't think you'd want him to run away."

"I didn't want him outside." Eden knelt down and inspected the collar. It was new, black and spiked. A dog collar, she realized. It figured. "He's not safe outside," she added, and quickly unsnapped it from the lead.

"He's not safe inside. And if he uses my drafting table for a scratching post again, I'll do more than tie him to the pillar next time."

Eden pulled Rocky into her lap. "You don't like cats, do you?"

"No," he said, and closed his eyes.

"Well, don't feel you have to hold back on my account," she muttered and carried Rocky to the door.

"Do you know he misses you? Sat at the window all day, watching for you."

"He was watching for birds," Eden said dryly and set the cat inside. "Rocky and I have a long-standing agreement. I don't ask where he's been and he doesn't ask where I'm going. Works out fine for both of us."

She closed the door, then turned back to Steve. "So what exactly are you doing now?"

"Practicing." He folded his arms and settled a little deeper into the corner. "First time I ever set foot on this porch, I knew this would be the perfect spot for a hammock." He opened one eye and smiled. "And I was right."

"Well, don't start banging in any nails yet. This is far from over." She shoved a hand into her pocket and pulled out the card Joanne had given her. "We have a command performance next week with a wedding planner." She dropped the card into his lap. "Courtesy of Helen Cormier."

While he read the card, Eden stood close enough to detect the fresh scents of soap and shampoo. His hair was still damp and he'd changed, too, she realized, taking in the loose fitting khakis and fresh shirt, and suddenly aware of how wilted and dirty she must look.

Steve held out the card. "We don't have to go."

"Of course we do." She snatched the card from his hand, wanting nothing more than a shower and finding it very satisfying to blame him because there was none. "Helen went to a lot of trouble to get that appointment. If we don't show up, how will it look?"

"Like we want to be left alone?"

"Very funny."

"I'm serious." He sat up and pulled a cigarette from the pack on the railing beside him. Placing it between his lips, he slapped his pockets, searching for a match. "All we do is thank Helen and explain that while we appreciate the gesture, we don't have time."

"You don't know how determined she is to get involved in this wedding. Not to mention the rest of the town as well. I'm beginning to wish I'd never heard of Kilbride." She stared at the cigarette. "Do you have to do that?"

"You mean smoke?" Steve took the cigarette from his mouth and examined it. "Yes, I believe I do."

"Then can you do it somewhere else?"

His eyes never left hers as he found the matches and flipped the pack open. "Bothers you, does it?"

"You're very perceptive." She sank down on the step. "Suffice to say that everything about it offends me."

"Understandable." He lit the cigarette, his eyes narrowing against the smoke as he studied her. "How long since you quit?"

She turned slowly to face him. "I beg your pardon."

"Just curious." His lips curled around the cigarette again.

She didn't know which was worse—his knowing or her

need. She plunked her elbows on her knees and cupped her face in her hands. "Six months, three weeks, five days, not counting the weekend my purse was stolen." She shot him a sideways glance. "It's been hard, okay, and right now my habit is out there doing push-ups in Helen Cormier's backyard, just waiting for me to weaken. But I'm determined to make it this time."

"Then in honor of your struggle, we'll declare this a smoke-free environment." He rose, took one last drag, dropped the butt and crushed it beneath his heel. "Easier now?"

She turned away, surprised he'd been so reasonable. "Yes, thank you."

"Good," he said and sat on the railing again, stretching his legs out and closing his eyes. "Now tell me about this wedding planner."

Glad to have something to focus her anger on again, Eden explained about running into the Historical Board in the bar, carefully skirting the issue of her video and the possibility of lineups at the door. There would be plenty of time to tell him later. If she had to.

So she told him about the developer and the fraud charges and Joanne's insistence that she and Helen help with the wedding plans. "It's as though they want to be my mother," she concluded and slumped against the post.

"After the prison story, who can blame them?"

Eden sighed. "All right so I went over the top on that one, and I promise I'll keep a low profile from here on in. But it won't help us with the wedding planner. Or Helen's party next Saturday night."

"The party is easy," he said. "I have to go back to Ohio for a few days anyway. I'll make sure it includes that Saturday and we don't let her pin us down to another date. As for Featherstone's, we put in an appearance and get out again.'' He slid off the railing. ''As long as we work together, we'll be fine.''

She raised a brow. ''Like partners?''

He smiled. ''Something like that.''

Eden watched him come toward her, and she had to admit he was really quite appealing when he wasn't playing king of the castle.

He sat down next to her and reached for her hand. She started to pull away but he twined his fingers with hers, whispering. ''We've got an audience.''

Eden followed his gaze. The couple across the road were snuggled together on the porch swing, gently rocking back and forth, oblivious to anything but each other.

She turned back to Steve. ''I don't think they're looking at us.''

He lifted her hand and brushed his lips across her knuckles. ''You want to risk it?''

Her voice when it came was no more than a whisper, ''I guess not.''

He nodded and settled back against the post, taking her with him. He moved her between his legs, easing her back against his chest. Eden stiffened, wanting to pull away, needing to stay. And finally taking her lead from the couple on the swing, telling herself it would look bad if she moved off now.

The silence stretched out, not awkwardly as she'd expected, but easily, comfortably, and she let herself relax, feeling the breeze on her skin and the warmth at her back. Enjoying the way his arms went around her when she shivered and his fingers twined with hers, holding them still when they would have drummed and fidgeted.

The streetlights came alive and crickets stirred in the grass. A few early stars flickered overhead, somewhere a dog barked, and Helen and the Board seemed very far away.

"I took your things upstairs," he said at last. "And I kept the water hot on the stove if you want it."

"Thank you," Eden said and felt herself smile.

These were things he would do without thinking, she realized. Gestures as natural to him as splitting a tab was to Michael and most other men she knew—men of raised consciousness, who wouldn't think to carry her bags or open a door or give up their seat on the train. She was, after all, an equal.

But to Steve she was a woman first, a partner second. And Eden was surprised to find the reversal so compelling.

A baby's cry drifted across the road and she turned to see the couple heading inside, their moment over. There was no one left to impress and no reason to linger. Their moment, too, was over.

Eden freed her fingers from his and moved away, seeing the puzzled look in his eyes as she got to her feet. "It's getting late," she explained. "And I was hoping you'd finish the tour for me."

He opened the door, holding it for her and pulling it closed behind him as he followed her inside. "On your right, we have the front parlor," he said. "A fine example of Victorian artistry."

Eden turned in a slow circle, viewing with dismay the dizzying patterns in red and black, heavy wood trim and ornate plaster moldings. The only sign of life was a drafting table by the narrow window.

It was not new and sleek in shades of gray or tan, but rather an old clunker of scarred oak with battered legs. No wonder Rocky felt free to use it, she thought, but made a mental note to call a wood finisher once they left.

Intrigued by the blueprints laid across the top, Eden

rounded the table for a better look. "I always thought you needed an architect for these."

"I am an architect, was anyway, with a firm in New York."

She glanced over, surprised. "Why did you give it up?"

"I discovered I didn't want to design shopping malls and office towers." He smiled and walked over to stand on the opposite side of the table. "And I never did get the hang of corporate politics."

Eden laughed, seeing the cowboy again, the maverick who would never quite fit in. "Why didn't you just start your own firm?"

He looked down at the drawings. "Because I missed the hands-on part of building. I don't want to sit in an office or direct from the sidelines, and that's what architecture is about. So I started into restoration work in San Francisco and kept going, buying up houses here and there, fixing them up and moving on. It didn't make me rich, but I liked what I was doing, and that's the important part."

Eden cast a quick glance around. "And now you'll stay here."

He nodded and she watched his gaze move over the room. "Yes, I will."

Eden turned back to the drawings. The lines and measurements meant nothing to her. It was impossible, in fact, to tell what room or floor she was looking at. But she had no difficulty with the smaller sketches—the detailed drawings of a new screen door, the parlor still burdened with shades of red and black, and the sketch of the conservatory that existed only in his mind.

It was a soaring structure of glass and light—a sparkling crystal attached to the house. And Eden knew a moment of regret when she realized she'd never see it built.

Steve stood by the fireplace, wondering about the

shadow that had passed over her face, and damning himself for a fool at the same time. Just as he had when he'd been relieved to see her finally pull up to the house earlier.

She wasn't his to worry about, wasn't his to make demands of. As long as she didn't do anything to jeopardize the image, it was none of his business where she went or when she came home. In fact, the more time she spent away from the house, the better off he'd be. And when she left, there'd be no reason to miss her at all.

She moved toward the door. "Okay, I've seen enough, let's move on."

"You haven't seen anything."

She stopped, looked back, and Steve knew he had her. "Take a good look this time and tell me what you see."

She shrugged as she came back into the room. "Classic William Morris that must be preserved?"

"Other than that."

She raised her arms, let them fall, obviously at a loss, so he nodded at the door. "Take a good look."

Eden studied the door. Dark wood and a keyhole big enough to fall through—just like all the others, except for the carvings at the corners. She moved closer and stood on her toes for a better look.

Jesters, she realized, complete with curled shoes and belled hats, perfect in every detail yet each one no more than three inches tall. But these were no king's fools. These were the hecklers, the picketers, the lone voice shouting "the Emperor has no clothes." They saluted each other across the top of the doorway, all the while laughing—at themselves, the house, at her. And Eden was hooked.

"That's the work of James Rusk Senior," Steve explained. "There are six sets in the house, each one hand-carved, each one different from the rest."

Eden settled back on her heels and took another look

around. No more jesters. Disappointed, she headed for the French doors leading to the back parlor. "Why didn't you tell me about these before?"

"You seemed bent on finding Norman Bates' mother instead."

She gave him a bland look. "And I won't be convinced we're alone until I see the third floor. So have you found them all?"

He smiled, obviously pleased that she'd taken an interest, and opened the door. "No, but I will."

Eden moved past him into the back parlor, checking corners and windows, and hearing herself call out like a child when she found two more.

They crouched at the base of the radiator, pointing a finger at her. She moved the screen aside, then finally took it off completely, giving the little men light and space and letting them thumb their noses at the world.

She stepped into the hall and smiled. Godawful wallpaper aside, the old house had some definite possibilities after all.

She looked over at Steve. "You may have to rethink William, because this house is ready for a change." She grinned and as she brushed past him on her way to the stairs. "And if you ask the little guys, you'll find they agree."

"What do they know?" he called after her, but she noticed him look over at the pair in the back parlor and frown.

She slowed down when she reached the landing, checking door frames and getting down on her knees to study the baseboards. She heard Steve on the stairs when she reached her room.

"I bought you something," he said and she followed him into the bathroom. "To make up for the shower."

He pulled a small blue bottle from the medicine chest.

"Bubbles," he said, setting it in her hand. "Because I couldn't find a feathered wrap."

Eden unscrewed the cap and lifted it to her nose. "Vanilla," she said, touched that he'd bothered to notice. She looked up at him. "Thank you," she said softly. His hair was almost dry now. Thick dark strands fell into his eyes, and he raised a hand, sweeping it back in one impatient gesture while his mouth, usually so wide and generous, tightened, making her want to reach out, to touch that tender lower lip with her fingertip.

And what would it hurt? she asked herself, to just let the longing take over? To kiss him the way she wanted, discovering again the taste that had been on her mind all day, knowing she ran the risk of never being able to forget?

As though reading her mind, he took the bottle from her hand and slipped an arm around her waist, drawing her in. And she went to him, her bones already liquid as she circled her arms around his neck.

She'd starved her heart for so long, she'd assumed herself immune to anything this hot, this sudden. Who would have known a man with watchful eyes and callused hands would prove her wrong?

He bent to her then, taking her up as his mouth covered hers, his tongue coaxing her lips to part, to let him inside. He deepened the kiss and she clung to him, lost in that place where sane voices were hard to hear and harder still to heed.

On a moan, he moved her back against the wall, his hands seeking skin as his lips moved over her face, her throat. And still she held on, breathing his scent and hearing his voice, so low, so sweet in her ear, a voice made for love, whispering her name as he pressed his hips to hers, slowly, rhythmically, hinting at what was to follow—if she let it.

Never had she wanted like this, needed like this. And never had it been harder to say no. But she'd only be fooling herself if she didn't.

She braced her hands against his shoulders. "No more," she said, the words sounding breathless and needy and convincing neither of them. "I want you to stop," she said, more clearly this time, making him raise his head, look at her.

He said nothing but in his eyes the questions were sharp, focused. And because she had no answer beyond fear, she kept silent and went into her room and closed the door. And was oddly disappointed when she heard him walk away.

8

Steve hopped on one foot while he pulled his jeans over the other, his agitation growing stronger each time he looked out his bedroom window.

Patience, he knew, had never been his strong point. And after three wasted days in Ohio and a red-eye flight home for the Featherstone appointment, his was stretched to the limit. But opinions of his ex-wife aside, he still considered himself a reasonable man. He asked nothing of anyone that he wouldn't give himself, liked a certain level of order on the job site, and expected simple rules to be followed. Rules of safety, for instance.

She was up there on the scaffold, top rungs of course, interviewing the soon-to-be-unemployed roofer. Her voice drifted on a breeze scented with honeysuckle, lilac, fresh-cut grass—"Chin up a little, Gerry, that's it. Now tell me, how long have you been doing bonsai?"

Steve stared at the window while he buttoned his shirt. Gerry did bonsai? In all the conversations they'd had, the roofer had spoken of baseball, wooden shingles and the merits of heat stripping over sandblasting, but never bonsai. Steve tried to picture the man with the sloping shoulders and the downcast eyes snipping intricately shaped branches with tiny scissors, and almost smiled. Trust Eden to ferret out that little tidbit and turn it into a ten-second video clip. And trust Gerry to fall for it.

What was the guy thinking about anyway? Steve wondered as he grabbed his boots and stomped down the stairs. But he already knew the answer. A smile so quick and brilliant it could take a man's breath, and a ripple of laughter that could steal his soul, leaving him groping and lost outside a closed door.

On a muttered curse, he growled at the cat, leapt off the porch and jogged across the front of the house. What did it matter to him? Let the roofer take his chances and be damned, but not until after Dorothy Elson's visit. Until then, Eden was his, for all the good it did him.

They had seen little of each other since that first night, what with him sitting at the drafting table until well past midnight and her all over town with that camera. Yet he knew she slept each night with a light on, ate cereal with marshmallows for breakfast and had at least ten different kinds of salad dressing in the fridge, every one of them red.

He'd hoped the trip to Ohio would make things easier, give him a chance to put things in perspective. But it had only made it worse.

Traces of her were everywhere now, from the cassettes and storyboards she left lying around, to the bottles of perfume, shampoo and cream that spilled over onto his shelf in the medicine cabinet. Not that he minded. If anything, he liked the way her scent lingered in the bathroom, the air sweet with that heady vanilla he knew so well now.

But he should never have left her alone. He rounded the corner and stopped, one hand raised to shield his eyes from the sun. She was up there still, a baseball cap on her head and the camcorder on her shoulder, nodding encouragement while the roofer talked and the rest of the crew tossed shingles into the Dumpster. And from where Steve stood, those didn't look like steel-toed sneakers she was wearing.

Steve's heart caught as he watched her lean back, only one hand gripping the metal bar while she followed the arc of a shingle into the air, oblivious to the fact that she was thirty feet above the ground and working without a net.

He walked toward the scaffold. "What is going on here?"

The roofer jerked around, his smile going slack. "Steve—"

"He's helping me with 'Kilbride, the Unexpected,'" Eden finished for him, swinging the camera around so it pointed at Steve now. "Smile, honey."

He pointed a finger instead. "Gerry, take that away from her so she can get down."

"It's okay," she called and turned the camera on Gerry again. "I only need a few more minutes—"

Steve moved toward the scaffold. "Eden, get down."

"As soon as I get this next angle—"

"Now," Steve said and put a foot on the scaffold.

Gerry wisely reached for the camcorder. "You better get down. We can finish this later."

"We'll finish it now," Eden said, keeping the camera from Gerry and an eye on Steve.

He continued to climb.

"What are you doing?" she muttered when he stood beside her.

"Taking control of the work site." He held out a hand. "Give me the camera and get off my scaffold."

Her chin lifted ever so slightly. "When I'm through."

The crew on the roof had gone silent, and Steve lowered his voice, reminding himself again that he was a reasonable man. "Do you really want to do this outside?"

She held her ground a moment longer, then tucked the camera under her arm and started to climb down.

He swung down a level. "Eden, give me the damn camera."

"I got it up here," she snarled. "I can bloody well get it down again."

On the ground, she raised a hand in a salute to Gerry and sauntered back to the house, as though the whole thing was her idea anyway.

Steve glanced up at the roofer. "You're fired," he said, then turned to those watching. "You guys want to join him?" he yelled and they scattered.

He glanced back to see Gerry already packing up his tools. Steve shook his head as he climbed the stairs. The best man he had, gone in the second week—that had to be some sort of record.

"It wasn't his fault," Eden said as Steve stepped through the front door.

He pushed past her on his way to the kitchen. "Gerry let you on the scaffold. It's his fault."

She followed him but stood in the doorway. "How can it be? I was out there taking some sunrise shots of the house when they arrived—"

"You were out there at dawn?" he asked, cutting her off. "Why?"

"Because I couldn't sleep." She waved an impatient hand in the direction of the yard. "The birds are so loud and there's only three weeks left, and now Helen has decided to hold a reception for Dorothy Elson." She blew out her breath in a huff. "Who could sleep with all of that? Anyway, Gerry and I got to talking, I asked if I could tape the guys working, and climbed up. It's that simple."

Steve hadn't heard much past the birds. And he didn't

believe for a moment any of those things had much to do with why she couldn't sleep.

"You can't fire him over this," she said, bringing Steve back.

"It's done." He jerked open the fridge, grabbed a container of orange juice and drank half. He looked over at her as he wiped his mouth with the back of his hand. "You want some?"

Eden's eyes narrowed. "Are you trying to be obnoxious?"

He gave a harsh laugh and shoved the container back into the fridge. "Honey, you haven't seen me be obnoxious."

She folded her arms across her chest. "Look, if this is about the other night, then get over it. We are roommates, not bedmates and that's not going to change no matter how mad you get."

It was the first time either of them had addressed that night, and now that she'd opened the subject, he wasn't about to let it pass. "Let me assure that even if you hadn't shut me out, I still wouldn't have found your little adventure on the scaffold any more amusing than I did." Steve slammed the fridge and gave her a long, leering look. "Only it probably wouldn't have happened, because you wouldn't have been in such a hurry to get out of bed if I'd been there."

"You arrogant—"

"You think I'm wrong?" He moved across the kitchen, each step slow, measured; carefully calculated to push her, to make her react, make her deal with him, with them, with herself. And he was absurdly pleased when she didn't back off.

Instead she met him head-on, eyes wide-open, her gaze

level and defiant, only the pulse at the base of her throat giving her away.

He stood before her now, broad and dark, and all she could see. He dipped his chin and a lock of hair fell into his eyes as he spoke. "Tell me you don't lie awake at night, wondering if I'm going to open that door. Maybe wanting me to more than you'd like to admit."

His voice was harsh, scraping across her skin, making the tiny hairs on the back of her neck rise. He was crazy, she told herself. Dangerous; a madman who needed to control everything around him. Yet wasn't that part of the appeal?

No restraint. She could believe that of him, and while she feared it, she knew that was what she craved most. To stop thinking and just feel, just be. No restraint. But always the warning was there, shriveling that part of herself that would have taken the risk. This is a fantasy, it told her. A game, a charade. But the one thing it wasn't, was real.

"Tell me you don't think about me, as much as I think about you." He reached out and stroked the side of his hand along her cheek, the tenderness in that simple touch so at odds with the threat in those dark eyes, she almost gasped.

He shook his head and a wry smile curved his lips. "Even you can't lie about that."

He turned away then, giving her the space she needed to breathe, to see the sunlight, to hear something other than the rush of her own blood. And she couldn't remember when she'd last felt so torn.

"But I want you to know," he continued, "as much as I want to make love to you, it has nothing to do with why I fired Gerry. As the general contractor, I'm responsible for everything that happens on the work site. And my insurance doesn't make allowances for stupidity."

"Stupidity?" She shook her head, reminding herself that this was the trouble with cowboys. "The only stupidity I saw was your reaction."

He rubbed a hand over his face and walked back to the pantry. "Eden, I was worried you might fall. And if you fell, I'd be responsible."

"No, Steve. I'd be responsible. And I'm pretty good at looking after myself."

He opened the pantry and studied the shelves. "So you've been on a scaffold before then?"

She slammed the door shut on him. "For your information, I have stood at the edge of the Grand Canyon to capture a sunset, hung from a helicopter to get a close-up of the Statue of Liberty and crouched in a hide in Kenya to get footage of a feeding lion. I think I can handle a simple shot from a scaffold."

He shouldn't have been surprised. Eden Wells was unlike any woman he'd ever met. Intelligent, interested, with a body that was firm, athletic. Obviously her life involved more than the sale of kiwis. He just hadn't realized how much more. And he didn't need to know. "Maybe so, but if you don't want anyone else to lose their job, stay away from my work site."

He grabbed his keys and portfolio from the table. "Come on, I've got an appointment with the Board and I don't want this thing at Featherstone's to run over. We can talk strategy in the truck."

She swung her canvas bag over her shoulder and followed. "Why bother? You'll just do whatever you please anyway."

"You're probably right." He saw the fire again, the defiance and almost smiled. As a couple, they would never make it. But God, the sex would be great. He opened the door and held it for her. "After you."

* * *

At Featherstone's, a wedding was more than a solemn vow between two people or a mere celebration of love, it was a business—and all three floors were dedicated to making sure no opportunity was missed. Invitations, gowns, tuxedos, shoes, lingerie, travel planning—there was nothing the staff at Featherstone's couldn't arrange for that special day. And nothing they wouldn't stoop to to make sure every bride wanted it all.

The air was scented with potpourri, the music just this side of schmaltzy, and business brisk. While the clerk in Fine China tried to mediate a pattern debate, the one behind the registry desk assured a long-suffering father that three hundred guests were not considered excessive. And the lingerie staff discreetly pushed the Merry Widows. A smile, a wink and would you like that wrapped, dear?

Scanners beeped, modems connected and thousands of dollars changed hands in the blink of an eye, all for a one-day event.

Eden stayed by the door, shaking her head as she took it all in. "A city hall wedding is starting to look better by the minute."

"It gets the job done," Steve agreed, "but that's about all you can say for one."

Eden glanced over at him, remembering the eight-month marriage. "Sounds like the voice of experience."

"It is."

There was no regret or bitterness in his tone. Yet there was something there, just below the surface, Eden was sure of it, and she couldn't help but wonder about his wife. Eight months with Steve must have felt like a lifetime to the poor thing.

But the opportunity to speculate was lost when an elegantly groomed woman came toward them, hand outstretched and a practiced smile in place. "You must be

Eden Wells and Steve Cooper. I recognize you from the paper.'' Her grip was firm, no nonsense, not unlike her hair. "I'm Arlene Vaughn, your wedding planner."

Her gaze flicked over them quickly. Assessing the budget, Eden assumed, and was curious to know where blue jeans and work boots sat on Arlene's sliding scale.

She motioned them to follow. "Everyone, of course, knows you're planning a September wedding in the garden. And while some feel it's a risk, I must say I agree whole-heartedly with your decision. That house has been scream-ing for romance and roses for years.'' She turned to them as she stepped onto the escalator. "Now I'm assuming you've already started on the landscaping."

Eden looked over at Steve, picturing the weeds between the flagstones, the iris creeping out of its bed and the tangle of wire rusting in what might have been a goldfish pond.

Steve smiled. "Everything's under control."

But Arlene was not convinced. "I hope so. Otherwise, I'll have to call in a few favors with my favorite landscap-er."

"Not necessary," Steve muttered, but Arlene was al-ready herding them off the escalator and directing them to the back of the store, setting a brisk pace.

"Usually I start with a tour of our store, but in this case, time is of the essence, so we'll go directly to the Wedding Countdown." She sent them a quick smile as they swept past racks of plastic-wrapped gowns. "Are you with me?"

Steve grunted, Eden nodded appropriately and Arlene kept going, taking them to a small windowless office beside the silk and dried flower arrangements. An antique desk and four straight-backed chairs sat in the center, surrounded by glass shelves and display cases, each one offering a taste of the selections to be found in Featherstone's different departments.

Arlene directed them to sit and closed the door. "This is the Planning Center," she explained, then checked her watch. "And we've got it for about an hour." She yanked open a drawer, pulled out a thick booklet and slapped it down in front of them. "This is your Wedding Countdown, the absolute cutting edge in wedding coordination technology. Do not lose it."

Steve leaned back, showing no interest in taking charge. Eden eyed him suspiciously as she dragged the book toward her. What did he know that she didn't?

Arlene settled into the chair on the other side of the desk and tapped her keyboard. "Now, if you turn to page one, you'll see we're already months behind in the preparation." She clicked a gold pen and held it out to Eden. "And this is where we start to catch up."

Eden reached for the pen, but Arlene didn't release it right away. "The way I see it, we've got eleven usable weeks. Twelve if you don't fall apart on me. But if we follow these guidelines to the letter, work together and refuse to be beaten, I guarantee we'll have a Featherstone wedding this town will remember forever."

Eden waited, expecting a band to play, flags to wave and hundreds of brides to march past, united in their common goal—the perfect Featherstone wedding.

But the moment passed and the music stayed the same. Steve checked his watch, Arlene tapped her keys and Eden wondered if there was a back way out.

"Section One, The Date." Arlene's fingers hovered over the keys. "I'm waiting."

"Third weekend in September," Eden said and sat upright, determined to get into the swing of things.

"Section Two. The Venue." Arlene looked over at her. "You'd better fill this in as we go along or you'll get lost. And I hate to repeat myself."

Eden scribbled the date on the first line and Arlene turned back to her screen.

"Write '16 Devon Avenue' on Line 2, then thank your lucky stars you're not trying to book a hall. At this late date, you'd be lucky to get the party room at the pizza place."

As long as there were no anchovies on the wedding cake, Eden couldn't see the problem. But she nodded solemnly and thanked whatever stars were listening.

"Okay," Arlene continued. "We need a minister's name for Line 3." She drummed her fingernails on the keys. "I don't suppose you've taken care of this already."

Eden shook her head, guilty again.

Arlene sighed. "All right I'll flag it, because until we have something on that line, we're going nowhere fast. Now the next issue, Line 4—The Bridal Party." She glanced over at Eden. "There's no time for a custom gown of course, but we've got the biggest selection of ready-made in the county, and tuxedos are always available. We can pencil you in for a fitting next Wednesday at five-thirty." She turned back to the keyboard. "And be sure to bring your attendants."

"There are only two," Eden offered.

Arlene's head turned slowly, as if not attached to her body. "Adults, or are we getting cute with children here?"

"Adults both," Eden assured her, relieved she'd got at least one thing right.

Arlene switched back to her screen. "Moving ahead to Line 5—The Tent." Her fingers stilled. "How many guests?"

Eden didn't hesitate. "Three hundred."

And for the first time, Steve spoke. "Are you out of your mind?"

"It's not considered excessive," she insisted, then

stopped. How many guests were low profile? She turned back to Arlene. "I was kidding. One hundred will be about right."

Arlene keyed the numbers into her computer. "Okay, here we go. A full list of tent suppliers, complete with sizes and prices for up to one hundred guests." She pursed her lips. "We should consider tables and chairs now as well." The keys clicked beneath her long white fingernails. "And a dance floor, platform for the band, one for the wedding party—"

"Hold on." Steve cut in. "How much is all this going to cost?"

Arlene just waved a hand. "We'll get to that later. Interferes with the energy when I'm planning. Now Section Two, The Caterer." She didn't bother to look at them this time. "Are we talking a theme at all?"

"Smoke and mirrors would be good," Eden offered.

Arlene's head came around and Steve nudged her under the table. "Or Ribbons and Lace," Eden said, figuring it was something the store did well.

"I meant a food theme," Arlene said dryly. "Italian, Greek—"

"Why not roast beef?" Steve suggested.

Arlene snapped her fingers before Eden could protest. "And Yorkshire pudding. That's absolutely perfect for the house. In fact we'll keep the whole thing very British, very Victorian. The garden, the decorations, the favors." She smiled at Eden. "Ribbons and lace it is."

Eden kept her face composed. "I thought you'd like it."

Arlene stabbed at the keys again. "Okay, all the best caterers are taken, as expected, but there's a fellow over in Shomberg who's available. Does a decent roast, although his desserts have never been wonderful. I'll put you down for a full course roast beef dinner, all the trimmings. We'll think of a fabulous dessert later. Something with flames would work well."

"The Martyred Bride," Eden murmured, but no one heard.

"How much?" Steve insisted and again, Arlene held up a hand.

"Details, details. Right now we need energy. Okay, on to the invitations."

The intercom beside Arlene went off and she snatched up the receiver. "Vaughn here." Her mouth tightened into a smile. "No, I do not think it's appropriate for her mother-in-law to wear a muumuu to the wedding. I don't care if she is comfortable…tell the bride to stop crying, I'll be right down."

She shoved her keyboard back and stood up. "Emergency in Mother of the Bride." She pointed past Eden's shoulder. "Invitations are on the table behind you, white binders. You pick one while I go straighten out mama." She rose and rounded the desk. "And remember, we are thinking Victorian."

"Kind of makes me feel sorry for mama," Steve said and reached for the binders.

Eden smiled and eased back in the seat, relaxing now that Arlene was gone. "Kind of makes me want to wear a muumuu."

"Why am I not surprised?" Steve said, his grin wide as he dropped the binders on the desk. "You take one, I'll take the other, and we'll get this over with."

Eden flipped through the pages of invitations. Hearts and Flowers. Two Become One. Share Our Joy. Nothing she hadn't seen before and nothing she cared to see again. But she didn't stop to wonder at the sudden restlessness that had her on her feet, needing to move.

"How about this?" Steve asked, turning the book toward her. "Think it's Victorian enough?"

Eden considered. "Roses, rings, cherubs, bows." She passed it back to him. "Arlene will be pleased."

While Steve ticked off Invitations on the Wedding Checklist, Eden wandered over to the shelves, touching a garter here, a feathered pen there. "You know, I've taped a lot of weddings in the past, but I never appreciated how much pressure those poor couples were under. I guess it makes it easier, though."

Steve's forehead creased as he flipped to the next page in the checklist. "From where I'm sitting, it looks like it makes everything harder."

Eden paused at a display of headpieces. "The process, yes." She leaned in for a closer inspection of a tiara, a double-decker special of sparkling rhinestones and irides-cent beads. Unable to resist, she pulled off her baseball cap, set the crown on her head, and smiled at the ponytail stick-ing through the top. "But it makes the real issue easier."

"The real issue?"

She set the tiara down, plunked a beaded Juliet cap onto her head and frowned. "The whole concept of settling down, getting serious, a mortgage for God's sake. All the things a wedding is really about." Resigned to the fact that Romeo would never have scaled that balcony for her, Eden pulled off the cap and picked up their copy of the Wedding Countdown.

"Take this, for instance. It's a perfect distraction. Keeps people busy filling in the blanks and ticking off the boxes, so they're not thinking about anything else. They're caught up in the tents and the tables and whether or not a seafood appetizer is a good idea, and never once thinking about the choices they're going to have to make afterward, when it's just the two of them and the fabulous honeymoon is over."

She tossed the Countdown onto the table. "Because if they did, the wedding industry would be in a lot of trouble." Suddenly aware that he was watching her closely, Eden picked up a nosegay of silk flowers and held it in front of her. "Just call me the Philosopher Bride."

"It's not you," Steve said, and she laughed.

"You've got that right. None of this stuff is."

"That's where you're wrong." He rose and walked her over to a mirror. "Close your eyes."

Eden's laughter caught in her throat. "What are you doing?"

"You'll see." He took the clip from her hair and smiled at her in the mirror. "Close your eyes."

"This is silly," Eden said, her voice growing soft as she felt his fingers moving through her hair.

"Humor me," he whispered, and she couldn't think of a reason not to.

She stood there, eyes closed, face burning, feeling ridiculous and special, wanting to laugh but afraid it would come out nervous and give her away. She heard a rustle behind her and he placed something in her hair, trying it first one side, then the other, taking his own sweet time as usual.

Then he laid his hands on her shoulders. "Okay, have a look."

She opened her eyes and he smiled at her in the mirror, and for once Eden had nothing to say.

She stared at her reflection, wide blue eyes, a sprinkling of freckles, and in her hair a simple band of delicate silk leaves, fluffy feathers and sprigs of tiny pearls, clustered like baby's breath on slender white stems. It was as insubstantial as a dream and just as compelling. "It's beautiful," she murmured, unconsciously lifting a hand to touch it, to set it in motion.

He bent down and whispered in her ear, "The Fairy-tale Bride."

For an instant it was easy to look into his eyes and let herself believe in gingerbread castles and happily ever after. Tempting to feel his warmth at her back, his strength on her shoulders, and think they really could fill a pantry together, or a china cabinet, or even a nursery.

He could build her a rocker and she'd put jesters in every corner to watch over their baby, and in spite of all she knew to be true, they could be happy. But after years of denial, it just wouldn't ring true.

She drew in a breath and pulled away. "I never was much good at make-believe. But I always enjoy a good joke." She took the headpiece from her hair, setting it down on the desk. "And this one is definitely on me."

He took hold of her arm and turned her to face him. "What are you talking about?"

"The joke. The wedding, the happily ever after, all of it."

"For us maybe, but not for everyone. And not for me." He waved an impatient hand at the feathers, the garters, the pink and white bunting. "I know this isn't what makes a marriage, but it's not a bad place to start. With a white gown, an engraved invitation and a hell of a party afterward, because it marks a celebration. Two people standing up in front of the world and saying, 'This I believe in. This I will fight for.'"

"But you didn't the first time, did you? How long did your marriage last, Steve. Eight months?" She shook her head. "Why did you even bother?"

She'd used it on purpose, knowing it would hurt, expecting him to lash out, to accuse and deny. And was humbled by his small, sad smile.

"We were young. It was a mistake. But I've seen love that lasts a lifetime, Eden. And I won't accept less."

She looked into his eyes and saw that he meant every word. He wasn't trying to sell her anything, it was simply the truth, his truth. And for the first time in years, she was jealous, because she knew he would find it. Just not with her.

He saw it first in her eyes, a faraway sadness, almost a longing, that had him reaching for her, as much out of instinct as necessity. And she moved into his arms, her fingers curling on his chest as he tucked her head beneath his chin. He stroked her hair, feeling the silk against his palm and breathing in the scent that he would recognize anywhere now.

He closed his eyes and tried not to feel the subtle rise and fall of her breasts. Tried hard to shut out the first stirring of desire that came from being too near this woman who was flighty and impulsive and only short-term.

He didn't want to learn the rhythm of her breath or the beat of her heart. Didn't need to understand the change of her moods or the source of her sadness. None of it mattered for what they were doing. But he felt her sigh, warm and soft against his throat, and knew with a painful certainty that he would never forget any of it.

She pulled away and he let her go. There was no audience here. No one to applaud and approve and spread the word that they were good together, perfect in fact. No one to fall for the lie, except maybe himself, and that was the last thing he needed.

Eden motioned to the checklist. "Fill in what you like. I'm out of here."

"Eden, wait—"

"I'm back," Arlene sang, opening the door as Eden hurried toward her. "So what did you think of the invitations?'' she continued, but the practiced smile faltered when Eden kept on going. She turned as Steve came toward her. ''We have other books.''

He brushed past. ''That's great.''

Arlene chased after him. ''I could drop them off.''

''Fine, and book the tent.''

''What about the caterer?''

''Him, too.''

''I'll need a deposit.''

Steve stopped, watched Eden get on the escalator and pulled out his wallet. ''How much? And if you say one word about energy, I swear I'll take this wedding somewhere else.''

Arlene moistened her lips. ''One thousand.''

He couldn't see Eden at all as he handed Arlene a credit card. ''Use this. I'll pick it up later.''

''I'll take care of everything,'' she called after him. ''And don't worry, this is just prewedding jitters. Happens all the time.''

''I'll keep that in mind,'' Steve muttered as he ran down the escalator.

———◆———

9

Steve stepped out into the street and the heat. The sidewalk was crowded with shoppers and browsers, couples with strollers and kids on a string, but Eden was nowhere to be seen. He walked slowly, searching doorways and shop windows, half expecting to see her coming toward him, appearing from out of nowhere, the incident already forgotten.

But he reached the corner and still there was no sight of her. It was as though she'd been swallowed up into the shimmering air—an absurd notion if he hadn't been thinking about Eden.

And why should it matter? The important things had been done. The myth of their wedding had been bolstered and the deposit made. No doubt the story of Eden's leaving would already be circulating, but so much the better. For all that Arlene tried to pass it off as prewedding jitters, Steve knew the first seeds of doubt had been planted, which would only make things easier in the long run.

Dorothy Elson's visit would settle the money issue once and for all, but however it turned out, Eden would be gone. And when the story made the rounds, people would purse their lips and nod their heads and say they'd seen it coming weeks ago. And if he hadn't seen the torment in her eyes or felt the tremor in her breath, he might even have believed she'd planned the whole thing.

He rounded the corner, nearly colliding with a bicycle coming the other way. He leapt to the side, ready to teach the rider a few survival hints, when he recognized the blond hair and the straightforward green eyes. Bicycle shorts and a helmet, the woman of his dreams on wheels.

She was already off the bike and offering apologies— just going in for lunch, should have known better, are you all right? Her eyes widened as recognition dawned. "The difficult guest," she said, and offered her hand. "I'm Debra." Her voice softened as she came toward him. "And you're Steve Cooper."

"Word gets around." Her fingers were cool and smooth, and he didn't miss the fact that she held on longer than necessary.

Traffic on the sidewalk parted and flowed around them. Strangers smiled, called him by name, and not one of them failed to take stock of Debra.

"In Kilbride, at least," she said, her hand slowly slipping away. She wore no scent that he could detect, nothing beyond the practicalities of soap and water to cloud the mind and blur the choices—the mark of a sensible woman.

She walked back to where her bike leaned against the store window. "You and that house have become quite the celebrities. And your fiancée, too, of course." She looked over her shoulder at him. "I hear you're going for a full restoration."

"Right down to the wallpaper," he said, and tried not to think of Eden dragging the jesters into her campaign to oust poor William.

"That's wonderful," Debra was saying. "It's always such a shame when people try to change those lovely old ladies."

Steve looked at her closely. "Old ladies?"

She nodded and unzipped the pack at her waist. "The Queen Annes. They've always been my personal favorite. So much charm and history, yet solid. A real family home." She laughed and pulled out a wallet. "I guess I'm just an old-fashioned girl at heart. Buy you a drink?"

Steve studied her strong features, her frankly sexual gaze and wondered why it couldn't have been Debra up on that barrel with a crowbar. An old-fashioned girl who dreamed of home and family and didn't mind buying a man a drink—exactly what he needed. Especially one who wouldn't run every time he touched her.

He glanced along the block, wondering what is was that could make a woman who scaled cliffs and snuck up on lions run so hard. He'd seen the transformation when he set the headpiece in her hair. For a moment, she'd become the Fairy-tale Bride, eyes filled with wonder, believing in love and happily ever after. But then those eyes had clouded and the moment was lost, leaving him alone in the fantasy.

He turned back to Debra, wishing her eyes were gray, or her hair touched with red. Wishing he'd taken her up on dinner when he'd had the chance, before Eden had moved in with her cat and her plant, and green eyes had faded from his mind.

"Another time," he said and backed away, knowing Eden wouldn't want him to look for her—and knowing he couldn't do anything else. "Enjoy the rest of your holiday, Debra."

"I'm here until Labor Day," she said as he started walking. "Maybe I'll drop by the house one afternoon."

"Great," he called back as he jogged across the road to his truck. "Eden would love to meet you."

* * *

It was nearly four when he turned the truck onto Devon and spotted her van in the driveway. Anger, frustration and finally relief washed over him as he pulled into the curb and shut off the engine. Of all the places he'd looked for her that afternoon—the park, the baseball diamond, the pub where her friend worked—it had never occurred to him that she might run home.

He yanked his portfolio out of the truck and stepped down from the truck. A simple message on his pager was all she'd needed to send—"Everything's fine. Good luck with the Board." Was that so much to ask? He glanced over to where her van sat in his spot. Apparently, yes.

He slammed the door. She'd been on his mind all afternoon, fleeting images that kept slipping in between the rational thoughts and kept him from concentrating, which hadn't made the presentation for the Board any easier.

He frowned, and slammed the door, recalling Noel's thorough inspection of each and every drawing; counting the number of walls sacrificed to modern comfort, questioning every fixture, every closet, every line on the budget. Within fifteen minutes, Steve had recognized the man for what he was—a pompous ass with just enough knowledge to make him dangerous.

Steve rubbed a hand over his mouth. The teeth marks on his tongue were probably the deepest they'd ever been, but at least he could congratulate himself on a job well-done. For over three hours he'd sat there, making notes of their concerns, even thanking them for their suggestions, and knowing he'd sell the house before he'd beg another nickel from that trust. Which meant this plan with Mrs. Elson simply had to work, because that house was his, and he wasn't going anywhere.

Deciding he'd earned a cold beer and a hot bath, Steve headed up the walkway to the house, his pace slowing as he drew nearer. Everything was eerily quiet. No hammers, no ghetto blasters—none of the comforting sounds of a well-run work site. He looked over at her van, irritation prickling the back of his neck. She wouldn't have sent them home early.

He took the stairs two at a time, only to be greeted by Gerry, shushing him with a finger to his lips as he stepped through the front door.

"Didn't I fire you?" Steve demanded. The man's shoulders grew straighter before his eyes. "I'm helping Eden," he whispered, then cast a quick glance along the hall and hushed Steve again. "And she needs us all to be quiet out here."

"All?" Steve asked and Gerry pointed into the parlor.

Steve slapped his portfolio into Gerry's hands and opened the door. Six men and women in business suits milled around his parlor. Some sat neatly on folding chairs, others stood mute by the window. And the only two he recognized were leaning over his drafting board, patting the cat.

"Jason? Anita?" They looked over and Steve stretched out his arms in a gesture of helplessness. "What is going on here?"

Everyone in the room shushed him as Jason and Anita each took an elbow and hustled him back out to the porch. "We're here for the taping," Anita explained once the door was safely closed.

"I assume you mean drywall," Steve said, then snapped his head around when he spotted his painter chasing a Frisbee out from the side of the house. Steve rounded the corner of the porch and bent over the railing. There on the grass sat the rest of the crew, calmly sipping his beer.

"Gentlemen," he said and they turned as one. "It's nice to see you enjoying yourselves."

"Go easy on them, buddy," Jason said, looping an arm around Steve's shoulder and, leading him away. "This all happened kind of spur of the moment."

Steve let out sound that might have passed for a laugh. Spur of the moment. Was there any other way with Eden?

"But she's almost finished with the interviews and the guys will be back to work as soon as Gerry gives them the sign."

Steve shook his head, confused. "What's Gerry got to do with anything?"

"He's my red light."

Steve felt a slender arm link with his, turning him slowly around. Her hair was still damp from the bath and she smelled faintly of bath bubbles and ice cream—a scent as intangible and sweet as a summer daydream. And just as impossible to hold on to.

"I don't have an official On Air sign," she continued. "So Gerry agreed to take its place." She gave Gerry a warm smile, but all Steve got was a dry peck on the cheek. "Members of the Chamber of Commerce have been coming and going all afternoon," she continued. "It's part of the 'Kilbride Means Business' video. And the back parlor makes a perfect studio."

She released his arm and headed back to the door. "We won't be much longer, so why don't you sit down and have a beer with the guys?" She paused with a hand on the knob and glanced over her shoulder. "Oh, and honey, when Gerry gives you the sign, please be quiet."

Steve turned to Jason as she disappeared through the door. "Did that sound like 'Sit Boy' to you?"

"Nah, you're just sensitive," Jason started but couldn't follow through. "Okay, maybe just a little. But she's got all these people here—"

"Not for long," Steve muttered and pushed past Gerry.

"Eden," he called, and all heads in the parlor turned. So he gave them a nod and took a slow walk to where she stood. "I'd like a word with you."

"I'm a little busy right now."

She started to leave but Steve put an arm around her shoulders, making sure she didn't go anywhere. "It'll only take a second."

Her expression remained mild, but Steve could feel her trying to find a subtle way to get free. So he tightened his grip, forcing her to make a choice. And it did his heart good to have her right there beside him when he headed out to the porch again.

"Gerry, tell the guys they can go back to work," she said on the way by. "Steve and I have a few things to talk about."

"And tell them I expect the whole south end of the roof to be completed before anyone goes home," Steve added and kept going.

"Are you being obnoxious now?" she muttered and waved to a passing neighbor.

Steve smiled and waved, too. "I'm just warming up."

Once safely around the corner, she jerked free of his grasp and wrapped her arms around herself. "Okay, what do you want?"

"I want to know what's going on in my own house for one thing. And I want to know why you didn't call to let me know you were all right."

"First of all, I'm working. I have a video to produce, remember? One that will cost me a fortune if I rent studio space. And second, I wasn't aware I had to check in and out."

"It's not a matter of checking in," Steve said. "It's a matter of courtesy." He took hold of her shoulders. "Eden, I've been worried about you."

She shook him off. "Well, don't be. I told you before, I'm fine on my own."

He took a step toward her. "You didn't look fine when you left Featherstone's."

"Everything okay down there?" Gerry called, and they both snapped around.

"Couldn't be better," Eden said as they both moved closer together.

"Just fine," Steve called, his smile matching hers.

Gerry nodded and went back to guarding the door.

"We're getting good at this," Steve said as they turned their backs on him.

"Very good," she agreed.

He saw her smile then, the tension easing. And it seemed only natural that he should loop his arms around her waist and draw her close. Only right that her arms should circle his neck and their hips should meet, pressing lightly at first, just testing, and finding the fit still perfect, exactly right.

And when she rose up on her toes, nothing would be amiss if he touched his lips to hers and tasted the warmth of the sun a moment before he deepened the kiss to find the heat that was hers alone.

But then the smile was gone and the fantasy over. She was stepping back, moving away. "Which just goes to prove, you can't believe everything you see."

She lifted a hand, gesturing to the front door as she started walking. "I have to get back. People are waiting. And I promise, I won't keep the crew off the job much longer."

Steve nodded and watched her go, knowing she was running again, to her camera, her work, all the places he wouldn't be. Which was fine, perfect in fact. And the next time he saw regret in her eyes, he wouldn't believe it. Part of the act, he'd tell himself. No different from their smiles for Gerry and their wave for the crowd. And when she left, he wouldn't worry about who was there to watch her on those cliffs, or listen to her laugh or hold her when she cried. Because she was just fine on her own.

He sauntered back across the porch, intending to work, something quiet, of course—God forbid he should make noise in his own house. But he paused at the front door when a nervous-looking woman with a microphone attached to her lapel emerged from the parlor.

He saw Eden smile and touch a hand lightly to the woman's arm, and while he couldn't hear what was being said, he saw the woman relax and laugh as Eden led her along the hall to the back parlor.

Steve followed, telling himself he owed it to the house to see what was going on, but hung back when he reached the door, not quite believing what she'd done. His back parlor was gone. No hardwood, no paneling, no stained glass. The walls and floor were covered with what looked like movers' blankets, bright lights shone from every direction, and cables snaked across the floor. Two cameras had been positioned on tripods and by the end wall, a single stool sat in front of a blue paper screen, and it was there that Eden and the woman stood talking.

"So the bells can be dangerous then," Eden was saying, paying Steve no mind as she gestured the woman to sit.

The woman twiddled her fingertips at him, then focused on Eden again. "Oh, yes. One wrong pull and that rope will lift you clear up into the belfry. Why, I remember the first time I tried…"

The woman rattled on, growing more relaxed as Eden adjusted lights and prompted her so gently, it was like two friends talking instead of the warm-up to an interview. And when Eden waved him out, Steve went, thinking of belfries and bonsai and barbershop quartets, and how he'd never expected to find any of those things in Kilbride.

Jason drew up beside him. "It's just carpet tape," he said, then nodded to the blankets on the walls. "The wallpaper will come down anyway, and there shouldn't be any damage to the plaster." He glanced into the room again. "I still can't believe she managed to create a sound and video stage, round everyone up and get most of the shooting done in one afternoon."

Steve nodded. "It's amazing what you can do on the spur of the moment."

"She's really something," Jason continued.

Steve glanced over at him. "I had no idea you knew her so well."

Jason shrugged. "She came by the Inn, wanted to get a few shots for the video, we couldn't just say no."

Steve raised a brow and Jason laughed. "Okay, I cornered her on the street and begged her to come over and give us a spot, does that sound more reasonable?"

"Much," Steve said and crossed to the fridge. "And I'm assuming it went well."

Jason hoisted himself up onto the counter. "Very well. She spent a long time with Anita, getting a feel for the Inn, the mood we wanted. Although I have to admit, her take was a little different from ours."

Steve nodded, imagining her going through the Inn the same way she had the house: taking everything in as it was, and then turning it all upside down.

"By the time she left," Jason continued, "we had some great footage and Anita had finally come over to your side. I even saw her look someone in the eye today and tell them she knew for a fact that you two were blissfully happy here and she was looking forward to the wedding." He pursed his lips. "If I recall correctly, it was Debra."

"So you've heard." Steve swung open the fridge door, more pleased than he wanted to be when he saw that she'd replaced his half-empty case of beer with a full one.

"Everyone has by now. Helen has quite the pipeline." Jason looked down at his hands. "Steve, I know it's none of my business—"

"You're right, it's not." Steve reached in and hooked two longnecks between his fingers. "I told you before, anything you see between Eden and me is a performance, all part of the plan. If it's convincing, so much the better." He handed one to Jason. "Anyway, even if I was interested, she is definitely not. She runs every time I get near."

"That's only natural," Jason said as he twisted the cap. "You scare the hell out of her."

Steve stared at him. "Well, that certainly makes me feel better."

Jason laughed and lifted the bottle to his lips. "It was the same when I asked Anita to marry me. She wouldn't answer me because she was terrified she might say yes."

Steve looked down at the bottle in his hands. "But at least Anita wanted marriage, a home, kids. Eden doesn't want any of those things. She's got plans, that one. None of which include me."

He looked around as Eden poked her head through the door and hollered to Gerry to give the sign. Steve watched her turn, catch sight of him by the fridge and smile, as though she was genuinely pleased to see him there.

Steve knew he could get used to a smile like that. Could let it light up his soul and become part of his life. But when it was gone, could he get used to the dark again?

"She definitely looks interested to me," Jason said.

"She's acting," Steve reminded him.

Jason shrugged. "As always, you know what's best."

"Yes," Steve assured him. "I do."

She ducked back into the room and he turned to Jason. "And I definitely want you to hang on to Debra's number." He picked up his beer and headed into the hall. "But right now, I want to have a word with Gerry."

Eden stood on the porch, her stomach growling as the last of the Chamber members pulled away. She could have taken them up on the offer of a late dinner at the Collie, she supposed—an evening with Nicole around was always good for her. But even the possibility of a free beer couldn't sway her. After a day of intense studio work all she really wanted was a little peace. She glanced back at the house. Odd that she would think she could find it here.

Turning away, she rested her hands on the railing and gazed out at the street. Not even nine o'clock, and she was the only one out. Unless, of course, she counted Helen, who was going to drown that poor rosebush if she watered it anymore. But Eden knew the angle was perfect from there.

If a person stood in that exact spot, and leaned over just a little, and stretched her neck to the left, the view of Eden and Steve's front parlor was unsurpassed. Steve at his drafting table was especially well displayed.

Of course it was easier from a crouch position with a zoom lens, but Eden figured Helen hadn't discovered that yet.

Eden dipped her head and hurried back into the house. Another minute and Helen would have been hotfooting it around the hedge and up the front walk, with yet another list of questions about the house and the wedding. Eden sighed and wandered along the hall into the kitchen. If nothing else, the woman deserved an award for perseverance.

Focusing on her empty stomach, Eden opened the fridge and studied her shelf, trying to decide if the best-before date on a tub of yogurt was really something to be concerned about, or if she should consider salsa a food group and be done with it. Reaching in, she shuffled the mustard, the mayonnaise, the ketchup, amazed as usual at how full a fridge could be and still offer nothing to eat.

"Didn't your mother ever tell you to keep the fridge closed?"

Eden didn't think about it when that smooth, familiar voice brought a smile to her lips. "Not my mother." She glanced over at him. "But Mrs. Kelly did often enough."

He straddled a chair and wiped the back of his hand across his forehead. "Mrs. Kelly?"

The gloss on his skin and the damp V on the front of his T-shirt told her he'd been working hard somewhere, and not likely the local gym. "The woman who looked after me," she explained and reached into the fridge, taking two bottles of beer from the case. "'Eden Wells,' she'd say, though it pained her so to say my name. 'Eden Wells, close the damn fridge.'"

"A woman of few words," Steve acknowledged, taking the bottle she offered.

"Always," Eden agreed, her gaze slipping to the chair beside him. They'd spent so much time avoiding each other that now she found herself on unfamiliar ground. Should she join him as any woman on the block might join the man at her table? Or had the day been complicated enough already? Maybe another late night at the Collie would be better after all. Keep the space wide-open, the edges smooth, so that when the time came, she could slip through without so much as a scrape.

If he saw her struggle, there was no sign in those dark eyes. He simply raised the bottle in salute, said, "I needed this, thanks," then tipped it back and took a long pull on the beer.

Eden watched him, thinking that even in this, there was no restraint. He was thirsty, he drank. He was hungry, he ate. And when he made love? She lifted her own bottle and refused to think further.

He set the bottle down and stretched out his legs, completely at ease, making her feel foolish. Perhaps she'd managed to push him away after all. Turned him into a roommate once and for all.

"So why did your name cause Mrs. Kelly pain?" he asked.

Taking a cue from him, Eden sat on the counter, curled her legs up into a lotus and relaxed. "Because it's a foolish name. Should have been Ellen or Enid—"

He froze, his beer halfway to his lips. "Enid?"

Eden laughed. "'Tis a fine Irish name."

"If you say so. So what did your parents have to say about it all?"

She shrugged and toyed with the bottle. "I don't think it mattered what she called me. They were just grateful she took me in."

He set the bottle down and leaned forward, resting his arms on the back of the chair. "Why would she need to do that?"

"They traveled a lot," she told him, because it was the easy answer. "And Mrs. Kelly needed the money."

His eyes narrowed and she knew he was waiting for more. But her stomach was growling and the story was long and she just wasn't in the mood to think about it. She slid off the counter and crossed to the pantry. "You hungry?"

He shook his head, letting the issue go as he sat back again. "I picked up a couple of sandwiches earlier. There's one for you if you want it."

She glanced over at him, more pleased than she wanted to admit. "What kind?"

He got to his feet and opened the fridge. "Steak." He pulled a paper bag from his shelf and held it out to her.

She wandered over, curious. "Don't you ever eat anything that didn't once have hooves?"

"I believe the lettuce is hoofless. You want it or not?"

She snatched the bag out of his hand. While he watched, she unwrapped the sandwich and took a bite. The steak was spiced, rare and tender. And she hadn't had one in so long, she actually heard herself moan.

"Hooves have a very strange effect on you." He leaned a hip against the counter. "Give me a bite of that."

She held the sandwich against her chest. "I thought you weren't hungry."

"I am now."

She held it out. "Just one." She watched while he took a bite. "That's too big," she hollered and snatched it back.

He chewed happily, echoing her moan and she laughed and kicked him with her foot, and saw a flash of what it would be like to be his wife. The easy intimacy, the smile that could turn from sexy to teasing in the blink of an eye. And wished everything could be just that easy.

She took another bite then handed the two halves to him. "It's too hot to go upstairs yet. I'm going outside."

He followed her out, carrying the sandwich and the two beers. He plunked down beside her on the top step of the gazebo and set the fresh half in her lap. "Eat," he said, then leaned his elbows on the stair behind him and finished off the other.

She ate, finding herself still hungry after all. Her gaze moved over the yard, discovering the place where he'd been working; digging out weeds, untangling roses, trying to put some order to the garden. He'd do it, too, she had no doubt of that. In his own way and his own time, he would make it exactly what he wanted.

She crumpled the wrapping and sat back, not full but satisfied for the moment. "I heard Gerry will be back on the job tomorrow."

"We reached an agreement."

Eden smiled. "I'm glad, because his salary was going to be a little steep for me to cover on my own."

He sent her a warning glance as he sat up. "So your studio worked well?"

She nodded. "The blankets always work in a pinch. With those and some good lighting, I can usually manage a pro-fessional-looking insert."

"What's that?" he asked, his gaze following the length of her leg.

She flipped her skirt down and sat up. "A static shot that gets inserted into the action."

She started to rise but he took hold of her hand and gently kept her back. "Eden," he said softly, "just sit."

He wasn't holding her with any strength. She could have drawn away, kept the space between them wider, safer. But if she let herself, she could almost see the peace she'd been searching for earlier right there in his eyes.

So she let him pull her down again, let his arm wrap around her as she turned toward him, leaning her head in the spot between his jaw and his shoulder; breathing in the scent of him, feeling the warmth of his body pressed close against her and hearing his voice, no more than a whisper against her ear. "You were talking about the action."

She nodded, feeling herself starting to drift again. "Without the action, it's all talking heads, which will drive people away from a booth faster than a live salesman."

He shifted, leaning his back against the post and moving her so she was stretched alongside of him. "You're obvi-ously good at what you do."

Eden knew she was going to regret this. She was getting

too comfortable, feeling too close. But he sighed deeply, and it was such a sound of contentment she couldn't bring herself to pull away.

"I like my work," she said, tracing a fingertip across his chest, outlining muscles the T-shirt only hinted at. "Not trade show videos, particularly, but I like the medium." She circled a nipple, watched his stomach clench and couldn't deny the answering tug deep inside.

He drew in a long breath that trembled slightly when he let it out. "What is it you want to do?"

"Classic poetry as music videos," she said, and laughed when he repeated it.

"That's the reaction I get from most people. 'Interesting idea, Miss Wells. We'll get back to you.' Only they never do."

She traced a lazy line up the center of his chest, felt him shift again and knew she was pushing, asking for more than a roommate. She laid her palm flat against his chest and toyed with the idea of just simply sitting up now, letting it go. But he laid his hand over hers, and she was trapped by his heartbeat, with no way out.

"So how will you solve this dilemma?" he asked.

"First," she said, aware that he'd moved again, turning his body just a little and laying her back so her head settled into the crook of his arm. "I have to make a pilot so they can see what I mean, starting with something familiar yet powerful, like *The Highwayman.*"

"And Bess, the Innkeeper's daughter," Steve quoted, bringing his hand up now to stroke her cheek, her chin, the fullest part of her lips.

"His beautiful dark-eyed daughter," Eden answered and reached up to cup his face, never finding him more beautiful than at that moment.

"And how do you see it working?"

"Perfectly," she said, but had difficulty seeing anything herself beyond the darkening of his eyes above her. "Period costumes, powerful new music, and a voice that makes you stop and listen to the words."

"I'm listening," he murmured, but she knew he wasn't. His fingertips were moving too slowly, too tenderly, sweeping her hair back from her face as though he could not see her clearly enough. And his lips, so close she could feel his breath, breathe it in and make it her own.

"Then I'll have to test it," she said. "With an audience."

"No audience," he whispered and she trembled as he lowered his mouth, expecting the same passion, the same depth she'd known before. But this time was different, as though he had nothing to prove and no need to hurry.

His lips barely grazed hers, kissing her so softly, so sweetly it made her eyes sting. How could a kiss be this tender, this enchanting, and not be real?

But the doubts were strong and the panic more so, making her draw back. He didn't try to stop her, didn't hold her hard or force her to feel what they both knew was building fast. Instead he lifted his head and brushed tiny, feathery kisses across her cheek, her jaw, her eyes, cherishing her in a way no one ever had before. Not parent, nor lover, nor friend.

And she heard herself sigh this time, a sound of such longing, such deep searing loneliness it shocked her, making her want to hide from it, from herself, but most of all from him. From this man who dreamed of crystal conservatories and chased down jesters and hated her cat. A man who was completely wrong for her, yet felt so very right.

He breathed her name and she felt the tension in his arms, the faint tremble in his fingertips as he stroked her hair, and she understood the effort, the care he was taking.

She reached up and this time the spark inside struck and caught, the flame holding just long enough for the thought to form—maybe this time. Maybe this time, she could leave behind the lessons of a lifetime and simply trust all the dreams and wonder she saw in his eyes.

He moved his arm around her now, lifting her to him, barely touching his lips to hers, making her arch to meet him, to seek him out. Then her fingers were in his hair, bringing him closer, her lips parted, anxious for the feel of him, the taste of him. And then his mouth closed over hers and she wasn't waiting anymore.

With long, slow strokes, he made love to her mouth, deeply, thoroughly, savoring her as no man had ever done, leaving her weak, breathless, straining for more. He lifted his head and kissed a warm, moist path to her ear. ''Let's take this inside.''

He was sitting her up, helping her to stand, taking her hand and leading her through the grass. And she clung to him, wanting nothing more than to follow him into that house and up the stairs. Past the dragon and the laughing jesters to his room, her room, any room at all, as long as he was there with her.

But the light in the kitchen was harsh and bright, bringing her down with a jolt. ''What am I thinking about?'' she said and pulled away. ''This is crazy.''

She heard him curse, saw his fist hit the fridge.

''What's crazy?'' he demanded. ''Two people making love in their own house? Believe me, Eden, it's the most natural thing in the world.''

He came toward her and she shuddered. It was all there, the anger, the hurt but most of all the need—the same soul-stealing need that swirled deep inside her even now.

She stepped back, searching for the space and finding the edges not half so smooth anymore. But if she stopped him now, she could still slip through, leave with everything she came in with, including her heart.

Drawing on years of practice, she managed a flick of the wrist and a careless laugh—indifference as an art form. "There's nothing natural about any of this and you know it. It's all make-believe, a fantasy. And I don't want any part of it."

He grabbed her roughly and backed her up against the fridge. "You want me," he said with quiet conviction.

She waited, afraid, excited, barely breathing, almost wishing he'd make a move, give her an excuse, a reason to run.

But she should have known he would never make it easy. And she almost cursed him as his fingers fell away from her arm and he stepped back. And this time he was the one who took the way out, who turned and walked to the door without a backward glance.

10

Eden hit Play and sat back, watching the opening sequence of "Kilbride—What Are You Waiting For?" over again. Music, a country toe-tapper, vaguely familiar but not intrusive. Flash to the ballpark—a guaranteed eye-catcher at a trade show.

Batter spits and swings. Crack. Ball soars, dissolves into fireworks. Military music, Fourth of July, sack races and hot dogs. Close-up of laughing faces painted red, white and blue. Ease back slowly, music mellows, softens into a single steady drumbeat. Faces are really a lone painting on the wall of the proposed art center. No more than a few seconds in total but the message was already clear—Kilbride was a great place to call home. But it still wasn't enough.

She reached out and pressed Pause. "Something's not right."

Nicole looked over from where she was misting George. "Eden, I'm telling you it's perfect. And if you don't come now, we'll be late for the fitting, then I'll be late for my first date with Deiter, and then I may have to kill you."

"Go and meet Deiter," Eden said. "The fitting can wait." She stared at the blurred image on the monitor a moment longer, then rolled the chair back and grabbed a handful of cassettes from the rack. "I need a different tempo for the ballpark."

"There's nothing wrong with the tempo," Nicole insisted, still spraying as she trekked around to the other side of the plant. "And you can't afford to miss another fitting. Helen is really milking the fact that you haven't picked a gown yet and I don't know how much longer I can keep Joanne from coming over for a heart-to-heart with you." She stood back and studied the plant. "You know, I never thought I'd say this, but old George is actually looking perky."

Eden glanced over at him. So it wasn't her imagination, after all. In the last two weeks, George's leaves seemed glossier, his branches sturdier. He really was starting to look, well...perky. "Must be the window," she said and went back to sorting tapes. "He didn't get a lot of sun in New York so I guess he's loving this." And she only hoped he'd be able to adjust when they moved back next week. "And you can assure Helen and Joanne and everyone else that I'll pick a dress," Eden muttered as she went back to sorting through the tapes. "Just not today."

The VCR clicked on and the mayor's voice filled the room, urging them to "Come on down." Eden abandoned the tapes and picked up a pen. "I've been wondering about this segment, too." She dragged a notepad toward her. "I think a different cutaway would be better—"

"The cutaways are fine. Everything is fine." Nicole slapped the spray bottle down on the desk and leaned both hands on the edge. "In fact, if you ask me, the only thing wrong here is you."

Eden bent her head and scribbled a few lines. "I just want it to be right."

"Come on, Eden. That video was right over a week ago, and we both know it. Yet you've spent every day since holed up in this room, fiddling with backgrounds and fonts and God knows what else. On top of which you are jumpy and bad-tempered and about to really tick me off." Nicole reached over and pressed Stop cutting the mayor off mid-sentence. "So are you going to tell me what's wrong, or shall I save us both the trouble and simply jump to my own conclusions?"

Eden put the pen down carefully but didn't look at her. "I'm fine-tuning. I do it all the time."

Nicole sat on the edge of the desk, refusing to be ignored. "What you're doing is hiding, and you've never done it before." She folded her arms and settled back farther. "It's Steve, isn't it?"

Eden dropped her head back and pressed the heels of her hands to her eyes, thinking that honesty was a highly over-rated quality in a best friend. And insight worse.

She banged her fists down on the desk and shoved the chair back. "Okay, you're right. Yes, it's Steve, and yes I'm hiding, and no, I'm not going to change my mind about him, so you can just forget it."

Nicole tipped her head to the side. "I don't remember trying to change your mind."

"Well, you would have eventually." Eden got to her feet and paced over to the window. "You'd think it was fine that he kisses me and I can't think of anything else for a week afterward. Or that he puts a stupid headpiece in my hair and I honestly start to think about happily ever after." She swore and kicked over a stack of bridal magazines. "I'm telling you, Nicole, the man is bad for me."

"I can see that," Nicole said, watching the magazines scatter across the hardwood floor. "So tell me about this headpiece."

"It's nothing, literally." Eden waved a hand above her head. "A few pearls and a bit of lace." She ran her fin-gertips down the side of her cheek. "And a feather that comes down just here..." She clenched her hand into a fist and crossed to the laundry bag on the other side of the room. "I don't want to talk about it."

Nicole slid off the desk and followed. "Okay, we'll talk about the kiss instead."

Eden pointed a finger. "We will *not* talk about the kiss. I'm sorry I ever mentioned it." She snatched up a T-shirt from the bag, rolled it into a ball and stuffed it into the suitcase that still served as a dresser. "We will talk about the weather, or the wedding or the house..." She snapped her head around. "Did I tell you I've found all but the last pair of jesters?"

"No, you didn't." Nicole knelt and picked up the T-shirt. "You'll only have to iron this later," she said gently, then sat down on the futon and smoothed out the wrinkles. "You were saying about the jesters."

"I found them in the tower, where I'm not supposed to go because the general contractor has decided it's not safe." She shook her head in disgust and thrust her hand into the bag again. "Took a while, but eventually I spotted them, lounging in a sunbeam, just happy to be left alone. Which I can definitely relate to."

Nicole nodded and laid the T-shirt into the case. "You get them on tape, too?"

"Miles of it." Eden smiled in spite of herself then, remembering the two little men lying with their backs against the door, arms folded behind their heads and caps drawn down over their eyes. If she'd heard a sigh, she wouldn't have been surprised. "When Footloose moves into animation, they will definitely be my first project."

Nicole looked up at her. "And if you don't find the last pair before Mrs. Elson comes next week?"

Eden shrugged and yanked a sock out of the bag. "Then I'll make up my own." She rooted around for a match, gave up and dropped the lone sock into the suitcase. "Right now, all I want to do is get back to my own apartment where I can use every shelf in the fridge and spread storyboards on the floor and feed the cat on the counter." She pointed across the room. "And not have to bloody well hum every time I go into the bathroom."

Nicole nodded. "I can see where the humming could drive you crazy."

"That's not the worst of it," Eden muttered and tugged her favorite shorts from the bag. The worst was not being able to sleep without seeing his face. Or breathe without catching his scent. Or think without wondering how different things might have been if she'd just followed him up those stairs.

The memory of his kiss began to build again, slow and inevitable, like the need that was always there. Eden gave the shorts a violent shake, then bent them over her arm. "The worst is knowing I can't just pack up and leave right now."

Nicole rescued the shorts and laid them in the case. "And Steve?" she asked lightly. "How is he coping with the humming?"

"Just dandy, of course. Hollering at the landscaper, fighting with the painters. It's business as usual. I'm the one who's going crazy." Eden reached into the bag and tugged on the sleeve of her denim shirt. "We haven't spoken more than a dozen words in the past two weeks, yet I hear his footsteps on the stairs and I know what mood he's in. I watch him tell Noel he'll take his advice into consideration, and know he's already forgotten what it was."

Nicole nodded. "That's what happens when you live with someone."

"Well, I don't like it." Eden yanked the sleeve harder and the shirt slowly unwound from inside the bag. "I dated Michael for a year and couldn't tell you what kind of toothpaste he used. But I know Steve uses that silly striped one, and that he shaves at night and that he likes to read in the tub.'' She shot a quick glance at the bathroom. ''I even know what page he's on in that book.'' She went back to tugging on the shirt. ''Although I don't know why he bothers. That book is so bad, if I was staying any longer, I know I'd end up losing it for him.''

As the shirt came free of the bag, Eden realized it wasn't hers at all. It was Steve's, the one he'd left on the bathroom floor last night. ''And now I'm doing his laundry,'' she groaned and dropped the shirt on the floor. ''Nicole, I have to get out of here.''

''Or maybe you have to stay.''

Eden almost laughed. ''I knew you'd say that.'' She crossed to the desk and sat down. ''How much clearer can I make it? Steve Cooper is not what I want.''

''No,'' Nicole allowed. ''But maybe he's what you need.'' She rose and gathered up her purse. ''I'll tell Arlene something for you. And I'll let you know how it goes with Deiter.''

Eden watched Nicole leave, and for the first time in her life, she envied her.

Despite all the heartbreaks, Nicole had never been afraid of love. She would laugh if Eden told her some needs are too sharp, too deep and some risks too dangerous. And she would never understand that Eden couldn't stay.

Not that anyone wanted her to. She glanced over at the door that kept him out, congratulating herself on a job well-done. Since that night in the yard, Steve hadn't so much as brushed against her in the hall. But if he tried again? She moistened her lips and turned back to her monitor. Nothing would change. She just couldn't take the chance.

James Rusk's garage hadn't housed a car in over thirty years, and Steve saw no reason to break with tradition now.

Since the moving truck had arrived from Ohio three days ago, he'd spent his time trying to convince the landscaper that formal borders were indeed what he wanted, and setting up his workshop in the garage—all under the watchful eye of Eden's cat.

Even now, Rocky sat glaring at him from the gazebo, just waiting for Steve to turn his back on the drafting table the animal had somehow come to view as his own. And if ownership was ever measured in cat hairs, Steve knew he could be in a lot of trouble. But with Mrs. Elson's visit only a week off, paw prints on his drawings and fur in his coffee would soon be a thing of the past.

With the cool of the evening settling in, Steve carried a pine board to the sawhorse, intending to think of nothing but the new screen door. Until he heard the old one swing closed.

He sat down on the workbench, tapped a cigarette from the pack and watched her come toward him. Her hair was down, her skin luminous in the moonlight. Her dress was a deep, rich blue, the color of the sky above her. With each step, the thin cotton swirled around her legs, defining for a heartbeat the curve of a thigh, the line of a calf before fluttering away, leaving only the memory behind. He set the cigarette between his lips, wondering briefly who it was she had dressed for.

She wasn't looking at him. Her gaze drifted from trees to flower beds, lingered a moment on the new flagstone path, then moved on, touching everything except her destination. Yet there was no doubt in his mind that he was her destination.

When she was headed away from him, her strides were long and her gaze steady. It was only when she came to him that she was hesitant.

He smiled ruefully and struck a match, cupping it in his hands as he lit the cigarette, wondering why it was that the one woman who made him feel truly alive was the one who wanted him the least.

He knew she would stop at the door to deliver her message, but not venture inside, once again making him feel like something that lived in a cave.

In the last two weeks, their public appearances had dwindled to the odd meeting on the porch to discuss some aspect of the wedding that wouldn't go away. Seasonal vegetables or salad? Silk flowers or fresh? At those times, she would stand near him, smiling and laughing, while Helen drowned the rosebush and watched.

Steve figured he was the only one who saw how stiffly she held herself or heard the edge in her laughter or knew how much she wanted to get away, which was fine. Because he was also the only one who knew she searched for jesters in the night, still slept with a light on and listened at his door when sleep wouldn't come.

She wanted him as much as he wanted her, he was sure of it. But she'd drawn the line and it was up to her to cross it first. And if she never did, then so much the better. It would make everything that much easier when she left.

So he pulled deeply on the cigarette to calm his breath, held the smoke to slow his heart, then snuffed out the rest to honor his promise.

"Why do you do that?" she asked as she drew up to the door. He looked over at her and she gestured to the butt on the ground. "Take one drag and put the rest out?"

He ran a hand over his mouth and strolled to the door making no attempt to be civil, as suited a cave dweller. "I gave my word."

She folded her arms. "But you do it all the time. On the

street, in the truck, everywhere. I just can't figure out why.''

He leaned a shoulder against the frame, deciding it was easier to level with her than to argue. "Because I'm trying to quit, too, but my habit lifts weights, okay? So if there's no other pressing business to discuss, I have work—''

"Mrs. Elson's lawyer called," she cut in. "There's been a change of plan. I thought you'd like to know.''

"Is she still coming?''

"Yes, but not when we thought. Seems she's cutting her safari short so she can join a cruise in Alaska. She's planning to stop on her way through, which will put her in Kilbride this Saturday instead of next.''

Five days. That soon. Steve stepped away from the door and walked back to his workbench. "What about Helen's reception?''

"I wouldn't worry about her. Helen's one of those women who'll make sure it's a 'good thing' even if she has to kill a few people in the process.''

"No doubt.'' Steve bent to check the measurement on the sketch, keeping an eye on the cat who had just come nosing around the door. "Thanks for the update. Don't let me keep you.'' He glanced over at her and had to ask. "I assume you're going somewhere.''

"Just over to the Collie. It's Poetry Night and Gerry's reading.''

"Dear sensitive Gerry,'' Steve muttered as he marked the cut on the wood. "Have a good time.''

"I will.'' She folded her arms and looked back at the house. "It's hard to believe we're almost down to the wire now.''

"That must make you happy.''

"No more than you,'' she replied and peered past him

to the rows of shelves against the walls. "So, are you going to show me your workshop or not?"

He raised a brow. "What about Gerry?"

"He's not on for a while," she said and glided past with Rocky right behind her. "And I should have an idea of what's in there so I can talk intelligently at Helen's reception."

He had to smile. It was either that or scream, and he'd so recently lost his status as cave dweller. So he turned and followed her to the drafting table, where Rocky was already eyeing the jump.

He heard her whisper to the cat and warn him away with a finger. And if she thought he didn't see her brush at the cat hairs, she was sadly mistaken.

"Still being historically correct, I see." She reached for the color chart clipped to the top of the table, tilted it up and shook her head. "Right down to the camel dung brown in the library."

Steve took the page from her and clipped it back in place. "I'm glad you disapprove. It tells me I'm on the right track."

"Or stuck in a rut." She picked up the sample of wallpaper for the parlor. "Any luck with this yet?"

Steve snapped it out of her fingers. "They're still checking."

She shrugged as she strolled away. "Suit yourself. But I'm telling you it's a sign. The jesters want a change. Ice cream colors is what I heard. You know, strawberry, peach, mint—"

"Vanilla," Steve muttered, and taped the sample down this time.

She glanced back at him. "You're thinking about it, I can tell."

Steve shook his head, positive she didn't want to know

what he was thinking about. But as she wandered off, he found himself looking twice at the camel dung brown, and wondering about strawberries.

"By the way," she said as she paused in front of his radial arm saw. "Have you found all the jesters yet?"

Putting the colors out of his mind, he walked toward her. "Probably as many as you. What did you think of the pair in the tower?"

He had to smile when she snapped her head around. "How did you know?"

He drew up in front of her. "You're not the only one who doesn't sleep at night."

"I sleep fine," she said, and continued walking. "I'm just curious about them, that's all."

"Whatever you say," he said, in a mood to be agreeable all of a sudden. "And to answer your question, no, I haven't found the last pair yet."

"Well, when I do," she called back, "I'll let you know."

She was standing in front of his tool rack now, studying the array of chisels, saws and planes that hung on the wall. And he wasn't surprised when she reached out to touch the ones that were different. "What is this?" she asked, already turning one of his saws over in her hands—the one with the double-edge, of course.

"A Japanese saw. Jason introduced me to them about five years ago." He walked over to stand beside her, determined not to yank it out of her fool hands.

"I was raised on power saws so the Eastern philosophy of woodworking was hard at first. But now I like the way these tools force me to get close to the work, to the wood. You lose that connection with a power saw."

"Steve Cooper and the Zen of woodworking." She looked over at him. "Who would have imagined?" She

lifted the saw, testing the weight. "I spent a summer working on a construction site and got to be pretty handy with
a regular saw." She held it out to him. "I want to try this.
And I promise to follow all instructions."

Then she smiled, and he hadn't realized until that moment how much he'd missed it.

Steve stared at the saw, knowing he should tell her no,
and realizing he would always tell her yes. He sighed and
rubbed a hand over his mouth. "Okay, but not that one."

He took another saw from the rack, one with a single
row of teeth, and led her to the horse. "Now take off your
shoes."

She eyed him suspiciously. "Why?"

"Because that's how it's done."

She kicked off her sandals. "It better be."

"Now stand on the board." Her mouth opened and he
held up the saw. "You want to learn this or not?"

Eden hesitated, trying to figure out if he was putting her
on or not. But those dark eyes were unreadable and his
expression deadly serious. So she gathered up her skirt and
put one foot on the board. It wasn't high. No more than a
foot and a half off the ground but it wobbled and she jerked
her head around to face him. "If I fall—"

"I'll catch you," he said so simply it was impossible not
to believe him.

He walked around to the front of the horse and steadied
the board with his own hands. "Now put the other foot on
the horse, beside the board."

Clutching her skirt in one hand, Eden instinctively laid
a hand on his shoulder for support and rose up onto the
sawhorse. She let go and stood for a moment, getting her
balance and enjoying the sensation of looking down on
him. Then she knotted her skirt to one side and held out a
hand for the saw. "Okay, I'm ready."

He smiled and released the board. "Not so fast." He touched a hand to her foot on the sawhorse. "Move forward so your toes are over the edge. That's it." He held up the saw. "Now take this in both hands, and bend over the board."

"You've got to be kidding." But he didn't look like he was kidding, so Eden took the wooden handle in both hands and bent over the board. She lifted her chin and realized she was no longer looking down at him. Now they were face-to-face. Her gaze found its own way to his mouth and lingered, fascinated by lips that were soft and full, and starting to smile. She bent her head and focused on the board again. "Now what?"

"Now you relax." He laid his hands over hers and she stiffened, but he didn't release her. Instead he leaned close, whispering in her ear. "If you don't, we'll both get hurt. Just trust me."

She nodded and tried to relax as he guided the saw to the wood. But he didn't start up high as she'd expected. Instead he set the top edge of the blade against the wood, then took hold of her shoulders, centering her over the board. "With this saw, you keep a light hold, use your whole body and feel the cut all through here as you make it."

A shiver ran through her as he ran his hands out across her shoulders and slowly down her arms to cover her hands again. "Now pull the saw toward you rather than push it away."

She kept her head down and pulled, hearing the ring of the thin metal blade, smelling the wood and feeling the cut in her fingers as the saw bit into the wood. She laughed and lifted her chin as she lowered the blade again. "You're right. I can feel the difference."

He merely nodded, his eyes dark and heavy-lidded as his

gaze drifted over her hair, her face, focusing at last on her mouth.

Eden felt her lips part as she struggled to draw a breath, knowing she should leave, but wanting only to stay.

"You want to try again?" he asked, and all she could do was nod. His hands lifted from hers. "Now pull toward you—"

"I know," she murmured, freeing the saw and handing it to him. "Don't push away."

The saw clattered to the floor as he wrapped both arms around her and swung her down from the horse. Her feet had barely touched the ground before he was drawing her to him, holding her easily with one hand, tipping her back as he cupped her face with the other.

Eden raised a hand, laying it against his chest, her mind racing, her blood already humming.

"Don't push away," he whispered, and lifted her hand to his lips, pressing a kiss to her palm, and she ceased to think at all.

Her arms rose to circle his neck, hearing the soft, low moan in his throat as he lowered his mouth to hers. On a sigh, she opened to him, her fingers curling into his hair as his tongue slipped between her lips, tasting, savoring, the way she'd wanted for far too long. But it wasn't enough, not nearly enough.

Rising up on her toes, she pulled him to her, sliding her tongue over his, dipping into his mouth; feeling herself ache and swell when he pulled his lips away and gazed at her, the hunger in his eyes pinning her down, holding her still.

Then his fingers slid around to her nape, turning her as he wanted, and he covered her mouth with his again, surely devouring her.

Freed by the very longing that had trapped her, Eden

clung to him, no longer motionless, rubbing her breasts against the hard wall of his chest, her leg against his thigh, loving the way he wanted her, the way he held nothing back.

Driven by a desire so naked and raw it was unlike anything he had ever known, Steve parted his legs and ran his hands down over her hips. Dragging her hard against him, he molded her to him, needing her to know that this time, there would be no turning back. And his control all but snapped when she moved with him, matching his rhythm, his need.

He lifted his head to see her. Her breathing was ragged and uneven, her lips still parted and moist from his kiss. The scent of her perfume strengthened and rose from her heated skin along with a musk that didn't come from a bottle. And the urge to take her there, hard and fast, was almost more than he could bear. But he forced himself to go slow, to make it last.

He brushed his lips against her ear. "You're going to miss Poetry Night."

Her lips curved as she opened her eyes. "I can live without it."

He drew back and she let her arms fall as she stepped away. But he grabbed her hand and held on hard, afraid to lose her now as he led her to the door.

The grass was cool beneath her feet, the light in the kitchen harsh and bright. But this time Eden hit the switch, and the dragon only smiled when they passed.

11

Her bedroom door swung open silently and the breeze ruffled the papers on her desk. Eden felt Steve's grip tighten on her hand when she would have hung back, taking her with him as he stepped onto the hardwood floor.

Moonlight slanted in at the window and the futon-for-one seemed to float like an island in the beam of pale white light. The rest of the room was in darkness and Eden's first instinct was to reach for the lamp. But he was already reaching for her, drawing her closer, his fingers pushing aside the slender straps of her dress, and the light in his eyes was enough.

Eden closed her eyes and just let herself just feel, giving herself over to sensation as his lips grazed a tender path from her throat out across her shoulder. This, she knew, was why she'd gone to him, sought him out in his workshop.

Later, she might tell herself differently, say it had been the passion of a moment, a fluke. But now the truth was all she knew. It was for him that she'd chosen the dress, fixed her hair and sprayed the perfume. And it was for him that she sighed now as she felt his fingertips on her skin, pushing that dress down so she stood before him, naked to the waist and waiting.

Her face was only half revealed to him, so faint was the

light in the room. But he didn't need to see more than the arch of her shoulders as he cupped her breasts, didn't need to hear more than her sharp intake of breath when he skimmed his thumbs over nipples grown taut and firm, to know she wanted him, wanted this. And he forced himself to go slow, to make it last.

He knelt, his hands resting on her hips as he took one rosy tip into his mouth, sucking gently at first and then harder as she tangled her fingers into his hair and held him fast, demanding more. His own control slipping, he lifted his head and pushed at the dress. "I want to see all of you," he told her, his voice sounding harsh even to himself as the silk slipped to the floor, leaving only sheer black lace to cover her.

Anxious to see, to touch the most intimate part of her, Steve hooked his thumbs into the band. And his heart all but stopped when she laid her hands over his, holding them still. Then she was kneeling in front of him, a smile curving her lips as she began the slow sweet agony of undressing him.

Steve sat back on his heels, breathing again as she took her time with each shirt button; slowly pushing it open and sliding her hands over his shoulders, his chest, his belly; coming close but never touching that part of him that ached for her.

At last he gripped her arms, growled a warning, and she grinned, shameless and satisfied, as she pushed his shirt off and kissed him deeply.

He took hold of her hands then and laid them on his belt. Her eyes were open, her gaze level and bold as she tugged. When the belt lay open, she turned to the buttons on his jeans; puzzling over each one and making him sweat as she dawdled and teased.

"Enough," he groaned, releasing the last button himself.

He got to his feet, taking her with him, then shoved the jeans down and stepped out of them. He watched her gaze drop below his waist and saw her take a step back as he moved toward her.

His eyes narrowed. "You're not going to get shy on me, are you?"

Eden shook her head mutely as he closed the gap, caught by the hunger in his eyes and lost in the gentleness of his touch as he pushed her hair back from her face and pressed a soft kiss to her lips.

"Tell me you want this," he whispered, his eyes searching hers as his hands circled her hips and his thumbs hooked into the lace that kept her from him.

Eden gripped his arms, her legs sagging beneath her as his fingertips brushed her skin, fanning a need that was already too real, too hot, surely turning her to liquid. Yet he waited, giving her an out, a chance to change her mind.

And when he bent to her again, pressing feathery kisses to her eyes, her face, her throat, Eden knew she could love this man. Not just with her body, but with her heart and soul. She could lose her way in the tenderness of his eyes, the heat of his touch and the wonder of his dreams, believing again in castles and princes and happily ever after. And when it was over? She'd find herself alone, with no way back.

So she held on to what was real, focusing on the scent of him, the feel of him and every nerve in her body that strained toward him. "I want this," she murmured, her voice breathy and soft. Then she laid her hands over his, easing the lace lower on her hips. "I want you."

She closed her eyes as he lowered her panties to the floor, and shuddered at the first touch of his lips. And when he lifted her in his arms and carried her to her bed, she buried her face in his shoulder and told herself this would be enough, because it had to be.

He laid her down in the sea of moonlight, trailing open-mouthed kisses across her breasts, her hips, her thighs. And then his hand was there, right there, where she longed for him; strong fingers stroking and circling, taking her to the edge time and again until she felt herself melting, into the bed, into him and a touch that could wring a cry from her heart.

Shaken, she reached for him, trying to pull him up, to make him finish, to make it end. But he took hold of her hand and kissed her fingertips. "Eden, please," he whispered. "Just let me love you." And she looked into his eyes and suddenly there was nothing to argue against and no way to resist.

Eden let herself take and Steve gave, loving her with his hands, his lips, his tongue; discovering what pleased her, refusing to stop, until she was limp and begging and holding nothing back.

Trembling now and close to the edge himself, Steve moved over her, settling himself between her thighs. Her eyes drifted open and for the first time in his life, he hesitated, wanting her almost too much.

It hit him then that he loved her. That this woman who climbed mountains and slept with a light on was the one he wanted to spend his life with. And she'd be gone in five days.

She was not what he'd planned, not what he'd imagined. She'd never be easy or pliant or practical. But her lips curved as she reached up, slender arms circling his neck, pulling him down while her hips rose to meet him. And Steve gave himself over completely.

Her eyes flew open and her hands gripped his shoulders as he pushed himself into her. Then she uttered a small cry, wrapping her legs around his waist and taking him deeper with each thrust.

He rose up on his hands, driving faster, harder needing to fill her completely, to make her his. Her arms fell away from his neck, stretching overhead as her fingers clutched the pillow, and he closed his eyes, arms locked as he arched above her, her name on his lips as he rode the wave of her climax to his own.

Exhausted, spent, but not ready to sleep, Steve rolled onto his side, tucking her in beside him. She settled and sighed, and he ran a lazy finger down the length of her arm, loving the way she looked at that moment—lazy and content, her skin flushed and heated, still damp from their love-making. And knew it was far from over.

"Eden," he whispered, his breath calming, his heart slowing. "We're being watched."

"Helen," she muttered and sat bolt upright, fumbling for the sheet and yanking it up to her neck.

"No, Rocky," Steve said, snapping the sheet away from her and tossing it out of reach. "He's at the door."

At the sound of voices, Rocky howled, raising the hair on the back of Steve's neck. "Why does he do that?"

"Because he's a pure-bred Oriental," Eden said, laughing as she threw her legs over the side. "And you're in his spot."

Steve glanced down at the pillow, his nose suddenly itchy. "Well, tell him not to worry. This wasn't going to work anyway."

"I didn't imagine it would," she said softly, then lifted the cat into her arms and turned her back on him. "You know the way out."

Steve cursed softly and got to his feet. "Eden, I didn't mean us." He laid his hands on her shoulders, making her face him. "I meant the futon." He gestured toward her bed. "You don't honestly expect the two of us to sleep there."

She held the cat tighter, already slipping away. "I never expect anything."

He saw the truth of it in her eyes and felt his heart squeeze. "Well, maybe it's time you did."

She crossed the room and set the cat on the pillow. "And what exactly would I expect? A declaration of love? Eternal devotion, perhaps?" She gave a harsh laugh as she walked to the closet and pulled out her robe. "I'm not that naive."

"And if I offered you both right now, what would you say?"

She held her breath for a moment but wouldn't look back. "I'd want to know if you're serious."

"Definitely."

Eden shoved her arms into the robe and belted it tightly. "Then I'd say you got caught up in the moment. Either that or you're falling for the lie just like everyone else."

"And if I told you you were wrong?"

She pushed a hand through her hair and looked away, refusing to hope. "Then I'd say it was a mistake. You admitted yourself you had trouble in paradise the first time around. Chances are you will again." She thrust her hands into her pockets and faced him, her eyes narrowed and dark. "You know, I've always been curious about what happened. Was it the smoking? Your temper? What exactly drove the little woman off?"

He'd seen this side before. Cold, fierce, protective. She reminded him of a cat caught in a corner. Confused and afraid, striking out at anyone who came too close, even the one who loved her. So he made up his mind to get closer, to risk the scars.

"I was nineteen when I met her, still living on the ranch in Nevada and she was just passing through. I married her in Las Vegas and followed her clear across the country, discovering there was more in the world than cowdung and cold. It wasn't until we hit Florida that I realized my wife didn't believe in monogamy.''

He watched Eden nod and turn away, the worst of married life confirmed. ''She had affairs.''

''Just one. I was away, she was drunk. Simple enough.''

''You couldn't forgive her?''

''Some things you don't forgive.''

He came toward her then, naked and beautiful. A man of high ideals, completely at ease with himself and the world. And Eden wished she had more time.

Time to run a fingertip over his beautiful lower lip, or trace the strong line of his jaw, memorizing each curve and angle to savor later, when this was all just a memory.

He lifted one of the ties of her robe, and Eden knew if he touched her, she'd be finished. So she backed up a step, but he held on and she felt the belt loosen.

''Now I'm curious about something,'' he said. ''Would you forgive a man an affair?''

She slipped the belt from his fingers and fastened her robe tighter. ''I wouldn't put myself in a position where it would be an issue in the first place. But hypothetically speaking, if I had a relationship with a man and he had an affair, I'd have to say yes, I'd probably forgive him.''

''Then you're a fool.''

''Not a fool, Steve. Just realistic, and that's the difference between us. You expect too much of love and will always be disappointed. While I expect nothing and am rarely surprised.''

''Did Mrs. Kelly teach you that, too?''

Eden almost smiled. ''No, that was something I learned from my parents, the summer they went to Afghanistan.''

She headed for the door. "I'm going to make coffee, you want some?"

He took hold of her hand as she passed, spoiling her escape. "Eden, where is your mother, really? Or your father for that matter?" He brought her to him then, holding her fast. "Where is your family?"

She raised a hand in a gesture of frustration. "Last I heard it was Burma. Now if you'll excuse me—"

"Not this time." He backed her up, sat her down on the futon and knelt in front of her. "Tell me about your family."

She rolled her eyes. "They're successful, they travel, they—"

He gave her a shake, stopping her cold. "Don't pull that with me, Eden. Not now."

She pushed his hands from her shoulders and stood up, needing to move, to put a distance between herself and the compassion she'd seen so clearly in his eyes. "What do you want? To know that I was a mistake? A lovely little error in judgment that seriously cramped the style of two free spirits who believed that the needs of the many far outweigh the needs of the few."

"The grand gesture," Steve said softly.

Eden turned and pointed a finger at him. "He catches on."

Then she was moving again, to the door, the window, the foot of the bed, being careful to stay out of reach. "Don't get me wrong. They were never cruel or mean, just absent. No matter what natural disaster they were devoting themselves to, I always received gifts for my birthday and Christmas with lovely cards that I kept for years because they had these notes on the bottom, 'Love you, baby. See you soon.' Only I rarely did."

Steve rose and sat on the futon, his fingers absently stroking the cat. "And that's where Mrs. Kelly fits in?"

Eden walked back to the futon and laid claim to her cat. Rocky settled on her shoulder and purred, too used to her outbursts to be rattled by this. "She had six kids, no husband and was the best thing that ever happened to me. Mrs. Kelly showed me that an independent woman can never be hurt. She put her faith in no one and had no patience for tears from those who did. 'Eden Wells,' she'd say whenever I was down. 'Just get on with it.'"

He rose and crossed to where she stood. "So you did."

She nodded and met his gaze. "I have work that I love, friends who are good for me and when this is over, a chance to fulfill a dream I've had for a long time. I'm happy with my life."

He reached out and scratched Rocky under the chin. "Militantly so, I'd say."

"When necessary," she acknowledged, and smiled on a sudden rush of affection for this man who knew her almost as well as she knew herself, and deserved nothing but honesty. "And I have no intention of changing."

"Then I won't ask you to." He took hold of her belt and untied the knot. "All I'll ask you to do is think about what I said."

Her robe opened and he turned, heading to the bathroom, crossing through to the door that led to his room.

Eden set the cat down and trailed behind. "There is nothing to think about," she called, stopping first to tie the belt, then stopping again to untie it, more confused than ever. She finally left it and walked into the bathroom. "Let's just enjoy these next few days and I'll leave while the memories are still good."

He came out of his room carrying the mattress from his

cot and a comforter. "Did Mrs. Kelly teach you that, too?" he asked as he passed.

"I learned that on my own." She followed him through to her room again. "What are you doing?"

"I told you it wouldn't work on your bed." He dropped his mattress on the floor, pulled hers off the frame and pushed the two together, covering them both with his comforter. "Until tomorrow, this will have to do."

Eden didn't know what difference tomorrow could make. But as he came toward her, she found she didn't want to think about it anymore. In fact, she found she had enough on her mind when his hands slid inside her robe and pushed it to the floor. And even less when his fingers cupped her neck and drew her to him so that clever tongue of his could make slow, sweet love to her mouth.

When he picked her up and placed her on their makeshift bed, she wasn't thinking about anything at all as he pinned her wrists above her head and studied her with eyes grown dark and heavy-lidded.

She felt her pulse quicken and her arms grow limp as his gaze moved lazily over her breasts, her belly, her hips. He drew a fingertip down between her breasts and the languor spread farther, warm and seductive. And she felt herself move for him, easily, naturally, offering in a way she had never done for any man, and smiling at the wicked grin that curved his lips.

Oh, he was bad for her, this one. Life would be simpler without him, without this. And as he touched his lips to her breasts, Eden lifted to meet him, knowing, too, that it would never be as good again.

12

——◆◆——

Morning came, sudden and brilliant, filling the room with sunshine and birdsong. Steve blinked the sleep from his eyes and smiled, feeling her still beside him, her head on his shoulders, her breath deep and even—the first night she'd slept without a light on.

She stirred and he propped himself up on one elbow to see her better. Her hair was spread on his pillow, a tangle of sun-gold silk that he captured between his fingers, remembering.

He'd felt the shift in her last night, the subtle change as each touch became more frank, more open, and she'd left the fear behind. He'd seen the fire in her eyes when she found what made him shudder, heard the triumph in her sigh each time she made him moan. And when he'd thought he couldn't last another moment, she'd shown him that he could, and started all over again.

He blew out a trembling breath, wanting her already. As he rolled slightly to kiss her, the mattresses slid apart, just as they had so many times in the night; forcing them onto one side or the other, an arm or a leg always slipping through the crack. And Steve knew the makeshift bed would never survive another night.

Her eyes drifted open and he waited, unsure of how she'd feel now, in the simple light of day. The thought of her running again made his mouth suddenly dry. But she smiled and reached for him, and he relaxed, knowing she wasn't going anywhere just yet.

"Morning," she whispered, pulling him down.

"Must be," he murmured, moving over her, needing her to stay, to be his wife, his lover, his mate. And knowing if he pushed her too hard, he'd lose her forever. She had to come to him in her own time, in her own way, and he only hoped he had the patience to wait.

She settled beneath him, sighing, opening. He touched his mouth to her eyes, her lips, the ticklish spot under her ear, and cursed the sound of the landscaper's truck in the driveway.

Soon the electrician would be at the door, along with the plumber and the plasterer, all of them ready to work. And for the first time in years, Steve only wanted to stay in bed.

Reluctantly he pulled away. "As much as I hate to say this, I have to work for a while."

She frowned and sat up with him. "How long a while?"

He got to his feet and held out a hand. "Not long. Why, will you miss me?"

"You wish," she said, but when she stood before him, he saw that she already did.

So he cupped a hand around her neck and covered her mouth with his, kissing her the way he would want to every morning for the rest of his life; determined to let her know without words that everything would be fine if she stayed.

He heard voices in the yard, tools being unloaded. But her body was too pliant and his blood was pumping too hard, and he figured the world could wait a while longer.

"Let's see how that tub works with two," he said, scooping her up and carrying her to the bathroom. "And this afternoon, we'll go over to the storage unit and pick up my bed."

Eden grabbed the door frame on the way by, holding them back. "What are you talking about?"

"A beautiful mahogany four-poster," he said and nuzzled his face in her neck, just below her ear, and in no time at all she was squealing and squirming and letting go of the door. "It arrived on the truck with my tools and a few other pieces," he continued as he stepped into the bathroom and kicked the door closed behind them. "I was going to store it until the house was finished a bit more." He set her down by the tub and bent to turn on the taps. "But I'd say we need it now."

"It's only for a few days. What we have is fine."

He glanced up and saw the practiced indifference, the small step backward, and knew he had to tread softly.

"Eden, it's only a bed," he said as he turned to her. "And you can leave it anytime you want." He smiled and looped his arms loosely around her hips, letting her come to him. "Although I guarantee you won't want to."

"You're awfully vain," she murmured, relaxing, moving closer by degrees.

"Just honest," he said and lowered his mouth to her throat. "It's a great bed."

As always, the kitchen was the hub of the work site, with a pot of coffee ready for the workmen who came and went with questions, work orders or problems for Steve. Dressed at last, Eden sat at the kitchen table, smiling and nodding and trying to form coherent sentences—all the while thinking that the tub could very well become her favorite spot. For the next few days at least.

Steve leaned down and set a steaming mug of coffee in front of her. "I'll only be a minute," he murmured. "Then we'll go get some breakfast." His smile was smug and knowing, and entirely too appealing. So Eden moistened her lips and smiled back, letting him know he hadn't bested her yet.

He chuckled softly and turned back to the plumber, but his gaze kept cutting over to her and lingering too long. And Eden took great satisfaction in knowing that he wasn't thinking about the materials list at all.

She raised the cup to her lips as Jason strolled into the kitchen with a wicker basket.

He held it and addressed the assembled group. ''Today I bring you not only the world's best blueberry muffins but tidings of great joy as well.''

Steve looked over at him. ''The oak for the cabinets is in?''

''Even better.'' Jason set the basket on the table and spread his arms out wide. ''My wife is pregnant.''

Eden wasn't surprised that Steve was the first one at Jason's side, his grin wide and genuine as he shook his friend's hand, slapped his back and finally hugged him hard.

''How's Anita?'' he asked, stepping back at last to give others a chance to congratulate the happy father.

''Great'' Jason said, smiling as he accepted good wishes and handshakes. ''Really great.''

When he was finally free Eden rose and offered a hand. ''Congratulations,'' she said, but Jason pulled her into a bear hug instead, lifting her off the floor and spinning her around.

''I had to get that out of my system,'' he explained, still smiling as he set her down next to Steve. ''Since I was too afraid to do it to Anita earlier.''

''Understandable,'' Steve agreed and poured Jason a coffee. ''So when's the baby due?''

''First day of spring.'' With just the three of them left

in the kitchen, Jason finally sat down. "I can't believe it finally happened."

"Well, enjoy it." Steve handed him the cup and slapped him on the back again. "So what'll it be? A boy or a girl?"

"Man, as long as it's not both at once, I don't care," Jason said and started to talk, about the baby, Anita, the nursery they were planning.

Steve picked up the basket of muffins and held it out to Eden. "Take one," he whispered. "Breakfast could be a while."

After she had pulled out a warm, fragrant muffin, he took one for himself, then put an arm around her and pulled her to him as he leaned back against the counter. Jason's brows rose but Steve prompted him with, "Any names yet?" and Dad was off again.

Eden glanced up at Steve, seeing the softness in his eyes and the tiny smile that curved his lips as he listened. It wasn't hard to picture him as a father himself—patient, loving, not afraid to be strict, but fair in the end. And always, always there.

Eden picked at the muffin, thinking about the offer he'd made last night. She had no doubt that it had been made in good faith, since that was the only way he knew. And in his heart, he probably believed it could last.

She could bake muffins and have babies and be the wife he'd always wanted. Or he could set up tripods and carry her equipment and be the husband she'd never wanted. But either way, they'd end up disappointing each other. And in time they would bathe alone, turn away from each other in bed and wind up saying things neither would ever forgive—and all because they'd expected too much.

So she'd do them both a favor and keep a space, and leave while she still could.

He looked down at her then, the love he offered so clear

in those wonderful dark eyes that Eden had to turn away, silently cursing herself for a coward and knowing this was how it had to be.

"Listen, I've got work to do," she said and reached for her cup. "Congratulations again, Jason, and give Anita my best."

She tried to break for the door but Steve stopped her with a touch of his hand on her arm. "You don't have to leave."

She saw Jason watching and quickly drew away. He didn't need to believe the lie anymore than Steve or herself. "Really, I have to finish editing that video. I'll see you later."

She turned and forced herself to walk, not run, into the hall and up the stairs to her room. She hesitated at the door, her eyes drawn to the scattered mattresses, the rumpled comforters, the clothes strewn on the floor. The air was still scented with the bubbles they'd used and the towels still sat where they'd dropped them, and Eden knew she'd never get any work done if she stayed there. Not that there was much to do anyway. As Nicole had pointed out, "Kilbride on My Mind" had been finished weeks ago.

So she grabbed her camcorder and headed back down the stairs. She cast a quick glance over her shoulder as she opened the door, listening to the sound of male laughter in the kitchen, and wishing she could stay.

Helen yoo-hooed over the hedge as soon as Eden's foot hit the porch.

"Well, isn't this a coincidence?" she said, hurrying around before Eden could make a dignified retreat. "I was just telling Tanner..." She turned around and shook her head. "Tanner Binnington, I told you to stay with me."

A blond head poked out from behind the bush and

woofed like a dog. Then the boy crawled out, wagging his bottom instead of a tail.

"What do you think you're doing?" Helen demanded.

"A pretty good Lassie?" Eden suggested but Helen was already marching back.

"Get up, for heaven's sake." She grabbed hold of his arm, dragging him to his feet. "What will people think of you?"

The child's eyes narrowed, then he screamed with pain and shrugged free of her grasp. The couple across the road opened their door. The man two doors down stopped clipping his lawn and Helen went very, very red.

"Tanner, stop this," she snarled as he staggered back, holding his arm aloft.

"Look," he shouted and turned a pitiful face to the street. "Look what you did to my arm."

More heads turned and Eden had to smile as he fell to the ground, rolling and groaning. The kid had talent, no doubt about it.

On a whim, she flipped the cap off her camcorder and lifted it to her shoulder. "Tanner, a little more to the right."

"Put that away," Helen snapped, but Tanner was already obliging, shuffling his body around and pushing his arm up to the camera.

"Tanner, get up this instant," Helen huffed and reached for him again. Then she shot a glance across the road, smiled, waved and backed up slowly. "Tanner, dear, perhaps you'd like to come inside for ice cream."

Eden didn't figure Tanner for a fool, and he didn't disappoint her. The boy gave Helen a withering glance, scrambled to his feet and headed over to where Eden stood. "Can I see myself now?"

Helen shook her head. "I don't think Miss Wells—"

"It's fine," Eden said, sitting down on the steps and

patting the spot beside her. If she had to choose between Helen and Tanner, there was no contest. "I'll show him the tape and send him home in a while."

Helen wrung her hands a moment, then shrugged and dropped them to her side. "Fine, he can stay. I only came over to tell you that the reception for Dorothy Elson is on for Saturday night at seven o'clock. My house, of course." She wagged a finger at Tanner. "Now you be good, do you hear?"

He ignored her and she turned her back, smiling broadly for the neighbors as she headed back to her porch. "Ah, kids," she called. "You have to love them."

Right, thought Eden, not surprised at all that Helen had none of her own. "Okay," she said, turning to Tanner. "You know how these things work?"

He glanced up at her as he moved closer on the stair. "You kidding? Of course."

Eden waited a beat, then set the camera on his lap. "Well, then I don't have to tell you that you have to look through here to see the picture."

She tapped the viewfinder and he nodded. "I knew that," he said and pressed his face to the camera.

Eden nodded. "That's what I figured." She pushed Play and watched him smile at himself. When it was over, he looked up at her, his eyes round and hopeful. "Can I do some more?"

Eden pulled the camera back and set it on her shoulder. "What'll we call it?" she asked.

He leapt off the stairs and struck a bodybuilder's pose. "Tanner the Great."

Steve watched from the doorway as the little boy strutted, danced, sang and did cartwheels while Eden conducted a star-quality interview. He discovered that Tanner was six, hated girls—although Eden was okay, loved school—but if she told anyone he'd deny it, and was in Kilbride because his mother was still mad about the contest. But Aunt Helen, it seemed, had a plan to fix everything.

Exhausted by the performance, the boy finally sprawled onto the step beside Eden. Then Steve saw her set the camera, the one that earned her a living, into his lap and let him view the tape himself, rewinding it again and again, to watch his own antics.

When at last he lifted his head, Eden popped the tiny cassette and told him she'd make a copy for his VCR if he'd like.

His eyes narrowed. "Promise?"

Eden held up a hand. "Promise."

The child's grin widened, and Helen's voice echoed across the lawn, telling him his mother was on the phone. Tanner waved goodbye and ran off as Steve stepped onto the porch.

"You were good with him," he said.

She shrugged. "He's not such a bad kid. And he'll probably be better now that his mother called." She turned her head and looked up at him. "How long have you been standing there?"

"A while." He sat down beside her, his gaze drifting over to Helen's front porch. "What do you think she's got planned?"

"A victory party for her sister, no doubt." She fit the cap on the lens and set the camera to one side. "But we'll find out for sure on Saturday." She glanced back at the door. "Where's Jason?"

"In the workshop borrowing chisels. With the cradle he's planning to build, I figure the baby will be about ten when he finishes it."

Eden smiled and rested her elbows on the stair behind her. "He's certainly happy, isn't he?"

"They've been trying for a while." Steve waited a beat. "It's not something you want, though, is it?"

She shrugged. "I told you before, I don't think about it. Which points to a horrifying lack of maternal instinct, indicating that I would not make a very good mother anyway, so it's just as well."

Steve thought of the way she spoiled the cat and pampered the plant and the time she had taken with Tanner, and wondered if she had any idea how ridiculous she sounded. It wasn't hard to picture her surrounded by children, tumbling with them in the grass, teaching them to climb, to take chances, to risk. And it was easier still to picture those children as his.

But knowing Eden, she probably believed her own lines, just as she believed nothing could last forever.

Steve had no idea what it was like to grow up without the love and security of family. Couldn't imagine what it had been like to be betrayed by the very people who should have loved her most, or spend a lifetime making excuses and pretending it didn't matter.

But as he watched her lift a hand and give Tanner "thumbs-up" as he followed Helen to the car, Steve figured he could make a pretty good guess. And the only thing he could think to do was to reach for her. To take her into his arms and kiss her right there on the street. To show her everything he was feeling, everything he wanted to give her. And let her know that all she had to do was take it.

Then he stepped back, watching her eyes open and seeing for a moment how much she wanted to believe and how hard she was fighting. And when he bent down to whisper in her ear, "Let's go get that bed," he had to race her to the truck.

13

Eden pulled the dry cleaner's plastic from her dress and searched out all the tags. Then she raised her arms and let the midnight blue silk slide down over her body, remembering the last time she'd worn it.

Sounds of laughter and music drifted in through the window. Eden glanced at the clock, then walked over to stand beside George, glad for the first time that the view of Helen's yard was so clear. Waiters in white jackets circulated with trays of drinks, the piano player kept the mood mellow and Helen played hostess by the gate. Arlene was already there, as was Joanne, the other members of the board, and Debra, the blonde she'd met at the Inn.

Drawing a deep breath, Eden wished she'd gone to Featherstone's for that fitting when she had the chance. It would have given them more ammunition now. Made the image stronger. But what was done was done. It was time to get on with it.

So she smoothed the dress and crossed to the bathroom, while the reception and all that it meant pressed in on her.

"I like that tie," she said, watching him form the knot in the mirror.

He looked over at her and grimaced. "Well, I can honestly say that I don't like any tie."

Eden smiled as he flipped the ends and pushed the knot

into place. She hadn't thought about how Steve would look in a suit. How the structured jacket would sit on his shoulders or the shirt collar touch his throat. But despite the fact that he didn't care for either, he wore them with the same ease and natural grace that he did a pair of jeans and a denim shirt, which didn't surprise her at all.

"We'd better hurry," she said, returning to find her shoes, her purse, the bracelet of braided gold and silver Steve had bought in Shomberg yesterday because he'd been thinking about her.

She slipped her hand through the delicate chain, doing her best to ignore the ache in her throat as the bracelet settled on her wrist.

She stepped into her shoes, tucked her purse into her hand and crossed to the bathroom again. "Mrs. Elson will be here soon."

"Almost ready," Steve said and pressed a kiss to her lips as he passed on his way to their bedroom, just another of the small gestures she knew she was going to miss.

"By the way, thanks for the book."

She glanced over at the paperback on the shelf. "I'm sorry I knocked the other into the tub."

"No, you're not. And to be honest, neither am I. The only good thing about it was that I was always out fast."

She smiled and went into the bedroom, standing just back from the bed. The sheets were rumpled, the pillows scattered and she couldn't remember ever being so content to never have a bed stay made.

While he pulled on his jacket and checked his wallet, Eden strolled over to the bed. He'd been right, it was a great bed, but nothing that she'd expected. The posts were tall, delicately rounded at the bottom, tapering to intricate brass finials at the end. A solid bed, yet subtly romantic, not unlike the man who had built it.

She picked up a pillow from the floor and tossed it into place. How often did they lie there, sweaty and exhausted and happy just to talk, little by little peeling away the layers to get to the heart? He'd told her about his family and the ranch. Explained how his parents had weathered everything from drought to floods and never lost track of why they were together. And she'd understood a little better what had shaped the man she loved.

He walked over to where she stood and pressed his lips to her shoulder. "You're nervous," he murmured, tracing a sweet, moist path across her nape.

"A little," she admitted, closing her eyes against the need to touch him, to hold him, to have him inside her with nothing between them and no need to hold back. But Helen was waiting and Mrs. Elson was due. This was the night they'd been waiting for. The only reason she was there. So she put a smile on her face and turned to him. "Break a leg," she said, and headed for the stairs.

"Don't worry about a thing, we've got you covered," Jason whispered, stepping out through Helen's gate as they approached.

Anita and Nicole stood behind him, both smiling and agreeing, but Steve hung back. "What's going on here?"

"You haven't been in there," Nicole warned, smoothing her hands down over her minidress. "Helen has got something up her sleeve. She's so anxious to get to Mrs. Elson first it's frightening. So we figured if Jason and Anita run interference with her and I chat up the lawyer, between the three of us, you should get at least a few minutes alone with the old lady."

"It's the only way to make sure you have time to speak to her before Helen can do any damage," Anita added.

"We appreciate it—" Steve started.

"No problem," Jason said, cutting him off as he pointed to the street. "She's here." He turned to Anita and Nicole. "Okay let's do it."

Eden stared as the two disappeared through the gate and Nicole headed out to the street. "It's good to have friends."

"If you say so," Steve said absently, his attention focused on the white stretch limousine parked at the curb.

A uniformed chauffeur opened the door and stepped back. Nigel Goodman, the lawyer, climbed out first, then reached back into the limo, holding out his hand.

A woman with thick white hair emerged, swatting at Nigel's hand and shooing him away as she stepped onto the sidewalk. She tugged at the jacket of her emerald green suit and pulled herself up to her full height and surveyed the street.

Eden leaned closer to Steve. "Do you think she's five feet tall?"

He shook his head as he linked his fingers with hers. "Not a chance."

They watched, fascinated, as the woman swung the strap of her purse over her shoulder and came toward the house. Her face was lined but her back straight. Her wealth was evident in the cut of her suit and the jewels at her throat, but for all that she moved with a regal bearing, traces of a cockney accent gave her away.

"G'wan, get away," she snapped when Nigel offered her his arm. "Bloody lawyers."

Eden glanced up at Steve. "I think I like her."

Steve squeezed her hand and started forward. "Me, too."

"Mrs. Elson," Helen sang, pushing past Jason and Anita to get through the gate.

"Eden, Steve, how lovely," she muttered as she hustled past, intent on getting to Mrs. Elson first. The rest of the party filed past, following Helen out to the street.

"You weren't fast enough," Jason said as he drew up beside Steve.

"There's plenty of time," Anita assured them.

Nicole just shrugged. "The lawyer's not my type anyway."

"Speaking of types," Eden whispered to her. "I thought Deiter was coming."

"His ex called this afternoon. Something about a lawn mower. But he promised he'd come by later."

Still believing, still hoping, Eden mused. And all she could do was wish her well.

"We're so pleased to meet you at last," Helen cooed, winning herself a cuff on the arm when she tried to take Mrs. Elson's elbow. "I can't wait to talk to you about what's going on in that house."

"I've heard all about it." Mrs. Elson stopped and looked Helen up and down. "Who are you?"

Helen smiled and introduced herself again. "Helen Cormier, Sylvie Binnington's sister." She gestured to the yard. "Perhaps you'd like to come into the yard and sit down."

"I've only just stood up," Mrs. Elson said, then turned to the crowd. "Now show me this Eden and Steve."

Helen smiled and pointed a finger.

The crowd parted and Mrs. Elson came toward them. "Young lady, I understand you want to talk to me."

Eden stayed close by Steve's side, already playing the devoted fiancée while they escorted Mrs. Elson through the front door of the house. Nigel had been left on the sidewalk with Helen and Joanne and the rest of the Board. As Mrs. Elson had said, it was a private tour.

Now she stood in the foyer and glanced around. "I hear you're getting married."

"In the garden," Eden said quickly. "The caterer is

booked, the tent is arranged and the invitations are ordered. I was looking for a gown but—''

Mrs. Elson looked over at her. ''You don't have to sell me, dear. It's plain as the nose on my face that you two belong together.'' Eden's mouth snapped shut as Mrs. Elson turned to Steve. ''What you do with that is your business. My only concern is the house.''

Eden and Steve stared at each other while Mrs. Elson took a few steps along the hall. She paused by the newel post, an odd smile on her face as she ran a finger along the dragon's spine. Then she moved on, touching a doorknob here, peering into a room there.

In the kitchen, she stopped beside the pantry and looked back at them. ''Show me what you've planned then.''

Never had the walk to the workshop seemed so long.

''What a beautiful cat,'' Mrs. Elson said when Steve flicked on the light.

''That's our Rocky,'' Steve muttered, sending a warning glance to Eden as he lifted the cat off the drafting table.

''Don't bother with blueprints,'' Mrs. Elson said when he started to pull them out. ''I want to see color boards and sketches of the rooms themselves.''

''I have no color boards,'' Steve said and pulled out the black-and-white sketches. ''But I do have this.''

Eden saw him reach for the color chart. But it wasn't his color chart that he showed to Mrs. Elson. It was the one she had done a few days ago, in ice cream colors, with a helpful guide indicating which room each chip was for, and a jester in the corner as a seal of approval.

She looked at him now as he laid everything out for Mrs. Elson. ''It's not what I originally envisioned,'' he was saying ''but if you keep an open mind, I'm sure you'll see how the house comes to life when you take away the weight of the past.''

Steve stepped back, holding his breath while Mrs. Elson studied the chart. He'd taken a chance and he knew it. If Mrs. Elson felt as strongly about restoration as the Board members, he'd be stuck with that trust for life. And he'd have to order the wallpaper all over again.

"It's very different," Mrs. Elson said at last, her voice softer than it had yet been. "Not at all what I'd expected." She pushed the chart away and turned her back on the table. "And not at all what James Rusk would have wanted."

Steve felt his stomach slide at the same time Eden's fingers closed around his.

"Mrs. Elson," she said, her voice suddenly cold. "May I remind you that this house is ours now."

Steve watched her face take on that look he knew only too well—the cat in the corner, only this time it was he she was protecting. And in that instant, Steve knew that she loved him.

"Eden, it's all right," he said,

"No, it's not," she insisted. "You love that house and I won't see you tied down, having to answer to the Historical Board all because she—"

"Did you know I was married to James?" Mrs. Elson cut in.

Eden jerked around, her mouth still open, the fury still churning. "I beg your pardon?"

Mrs. Elson smiled, ignoring them both as she strolled to the door. "I didn't think so. Few people did, and they're probably all dead now anyway."

"The woman is mad," Eden muttered, and Steve pulled her close, not wishing any harm to come to Mrs. Elson.

"It was during the war," the older woman continued. "I was an actress playing a nurse, he was a poet playing a soldier." She stood at the workshop door, gazing up at the house. "He brought me here when it was over. Told me his father built this house for generations of Rusks to live in and expected we'd settle down, start a family of our own. He didn't understand that I still wanted the stage.'' A sad smile curved her lips as she turned away from the door. "We never did see our first anniversary.''

Steve saw the ice leave Eden's eyes and when she pulled away he let her go, satisfied that Mrs. Elson was safe again.

"You went back to London?'' Eden asked.

"And James stayed here.'' Mrs. Elson put a hand to her throat, fingering the emeralds while she spoke. "I didn't make it in the theater but I went on with my life. Married again and finally had children. I never spoke to James again, but I always assumed he did the same. Then out of the blue, I received a notice saying I was sole beneficiary of his estate.''

She shook her head and her voice softened. "I had no idea he'd lived all those years alone, letting the house fall down around him because he couldn't bear to leave but didn't want to stay either. It was a cowardly thing, but after I found out, I couldn't bring myself to come here until the house was safely in someone else's hands.''

Eden's voice was gentle, compassionate. "But you didn't sell it, either.''

Mrs. Elson's shoulders sagged and for the first time she looked weary. "It was important that someone have the house because they deserved it, not simply because they could afford it.'' She glanced up at Eden. "James and I never found happiness here, but maybe the two of you will. And you're quite right when you say that this is your house now.''

Brisk again, Mrs. Elson marched back to the drafting table. "I agree it's time that the house shook off the past.'' She tapped a finger on the color chart. "Use your strawberries and your peaches wherever you like, only promise I can come back and see when it's finished.''

''Anytime,'' Steve said.

Mrs. Elson rubbed her hands together. ''Now I imagine you'll want to deal with this issue of the trust.'' She sent a quick grin to Eden. ''I wouldn't fancy being tied to that Historical Board myself,'' she said as she opened her purse and pulled out a set of papers and a pen. ''Whole thing was Nigel's idea anyway. Don't know why I even listen to him.'' She held everything out to Steve. ''Sign these, and it's finished. You can do what you want with the house and don't let nobody tell you different.''

Papers signed, she handed them their copies and stuffed the rest into her purse. ''It's been a pleasure, but I really must be going. Alaska calls.''

Eden glanced over at Steve as they walked back to the street. ''Mrs. Elson, there's one more thing I'd like to ask you about the house.''

The older woman's eyes twinkled. ''You're looking for the sixth set of jesters.''

''Why, yes—''

''Well, you'll never find them.'' A smile of pure delight lit her face. ''Because I stole them.''

Steve fell out of step. ''You what?''

''Popped them right off with a crowbar while he slept,'' she said proudly. ''They were his favorites so I figured he might come after them one day, but he never did. I'll leave them to you in my will, but you'll not get them before.''

''I hope we don't see them for years,'' Eden said, laughing.

''There she is,'' Helen called from the other side of the hedge.

The party had spread to Helen's front lawn, with small groups laughing, talking, sipping champagne. Eden spotted

Nicole by the tree, one hand looped through Deiter's arm, the other giving Eden a thumbs-up behind his back.

So he'd come, Eden mused, and a silly, romantic sigh escaped her lips.

"Oh, Mrs. Elson," Helen was saying. "I'm so glad we'll have a chance to talk now—"

Mrs. Elson held up a hand and kept heading for the limo. "Sorry, Heidi, but I've no time."

"The name is Helen," Helen said, trailing behind like a puppy. "And there are things you should know about those two. Things that just aren't right."

Mrs. Elson stopped at the door of the limo and turned, her eyes narrowing as she studied Eden and Steve. "I know all I need to know." She turned and pointed a finger at Nigel. "You want a ride, get in the car."

Helen stood alone on the sidewalk, staring after the limo as it pulled away from the curb. "I knew I should have met her at the airport," she muttered and marched back to her porch.

As the lights of Mrs. Elson's car disappeared around the corner, Steve wrapped an arm around Eden's waist. "What do you say we go steal back our jesters?"

She rested her head on his shoulder and smiled. "Somehow, I don't think we'd make it out alive."

"So how did it go?" Jason asked as he and Anita drew up beside them.

"Champagne, miss?" a waiter asked Eden. She looked down at the tray held out to her while Steve explained what had happened. Then she lifted her gaze to the crowd on the lawn and knew it wasn't time for champagne yet. There was still one more thing to do.

She watched Debra circulate, seeing her gaze slip over to Steve every now and then, knowing she'd probably be perfect for him. And telling herself the knot in her stomach had nothing to do with jealousy.

Dragging in a deep breath, she took a glass from the tray and backed away from Steve. "Do you think I'm blind?" she said, loud enough to draw a few curious glances.

Steve turned to her, not understanding.

"I saw you looking at her," Eden said, playing the part, getting it right, and holding back tears that were real.

"Eden, don't," Steve said, his voice soft, almost pleading.

But she knew she had to see it through, for both their sakes.

"Go to hell," she growled and threw the champagne at him.

She heard the murmur of voices, Steve calling her name and she kept going—from the walk to the stairs, up the stairs to the door. Squeezing the glass in her hand so hard, she was sure it would break.

14

Steve found Eden in their bedroom, her suitcase on the bed, packed, zippered, ready to run. She flashed him a smile as she went by on her way to the bathroom. "Well, that went well don't you think? Sorry about the champagne," she added and went through the door. "Send me the bill for the cleaning."

Through with patience, and waiting and holding back, Steve followed her into the room that had been hers. "Do you really think it's that easy?"

She was at the desk, sealing a cassette into an envelope. She shrugged, cool and indifferent, but her fingers trembled and she couldn't meet his gaze. "I can't see why not. It's what we've talked about all along. We played the part, got what we wanted. Now the only thing left is the money." She fumbled with a pen, scribbled a line on a notepad then tore off the page and pushed it to the side of the desk. "That's my account number. You can transfer my half when it's settled."

She went to her closet, taking out what was left—a shirt, a jacket, a pair of jeans he'd never seen her wear—and folded them over her arm.

He felt the panic rise and was beside her in two steps, grabbing her arm, spinning her around. "I can't believe you're doing this."

She shook him off and stepped back. "Why, because it's not what you want?"

"Because it's not what either of us wants. I love you, Eden. And I know you love me, too."

She shook her head and he reached out, seeing the struggle, the war within herself and needing to close the gap before she made it real. "It's right there, Eden," he said softly. "In your eyes, your smile, the way you look when we make love."

She lifted her eyes then and met his gaze. "I told you before, don't believe everything you see."

"Then I'll just believe what I feel." He rested his hands on her waist, easing her closer. "I'm not asking you to change, Eden, I'm just asking you to try. I'm not saying it will be easy, nothing worth having ever is. We'll probably fight and make up a hundred times over, but I promise I will never do anything to hurt you. And I will always be here."

She dipped her chin, still not believing. So he framed her face with his hands, refusing to be shut out. "You have to trust me, Eden. You have to believe in me. I want you to go out and turn poetry on its ear, or climb mountains or do whatever it is that makes you happy. And when you get back, I'll be here, because I love you."

He touched his lips to hers, a touch so soft, so tender it made her knees weak and her throat tight. He was offering her forever. The fairy-tale bride in the gingerbread castle. And as she reached her fingers into his hair and pulled him in, she wanted so much to believe.

There was no seduction this time, no endless pleasure, only a need that was too strong to deny and too wonderful to last. In a heartbeat she was naked and panting, and pulling him to the floor. She reveled in the hunger in his eyes, the strength in his hands and heat of his mouth on her skin.

And when she moved over him, taking the lead, gentleness and skill gave way to harsher needs.

The flick of a tongue, the stroke of a hand and they were both drowning, lost in a rush of madness, and taking each other deeper with each desperate cry.

Slowly senses returned. Arms and legs untangled. They rose and walked to their bed. Steve set the suitcase on the floor, Eden tugged the sheets into place. And when they lay down together and Steve took her in his arms, she pretended not to hear when he asked her, one last time, to stay.

Steve wasn't surprised to wake and find the suitcase gone. If he'd thought it would do any good, he would have shouted, begged, chained her feet to the floor. But she'd been honest from the first, and if he'd chosen to believe in a dream, that wasn't her fault.

He rose and reached for his jeans, the longing sharp and sudden, already missing her arms around his waist, pulling him back for one more kiss.

He went through to her room and his stomach tightened when he saw George and her editing suite still there. But a note on the desk explained that a moving company would come to pack up the equipment on Monday and George had simply refused to go. "Somehow he heard about the conservatory and wouldn't budge. He knows you'll take good care of him. So do I. Love, Eden."

Steve lifted one of the glossy leaves. So she trusted him with her plant but not her heart. How fitting.

Taking George's empty spray bottle with him, Steve carried on to the stairs, pausing at the bottom to look at the dragon, wondering if it had always had that smirk, then continued into the kitchen.

He sat at the table with his coffee and the plumber's

quote, trying to go over the figures again. But the house was too still, too quiet. No cat howling at the door, no laughter on the stairs, nothing at all to distract him. So he picked up his mug and headed to the workshop to make some noise.

He got as far as the back door when the doorbell rang.

"I don't normally interfere in these matters," Arlene said when he opened the door. "But when my caterer finds a message on his machine from one of my clients to cancel a booking, I just have to step in." She peered over his shoulder. "Now where is she?"

Steve leaned a shoulder against the door frame. "Eden canceled the caterer?"

"And the printer, and the party rental, all in the middle of the night." Arlene threw up her hands in a gesture of frustration. "What is that girl thinking about? Doesn't she know she can't go around canceling these things because you had a fight? Someone might take her seriously."

"I can see the danger."

"But then it's just like young people, isn't it? Least little thing and they're off to the lawyer, dividing the assets and searching for something better." She waved a hand. "Of course it's good for business. Used to be you got people once in a lifetime. Nowadays, who knows."

Arlene paused and came as close to looking thoughtful as Steve figured she ever could.

"But I still can't help feeling it's a shame when people give up so easily. When they let love slip through their fingers without a fight. I mean, it's not as though love is easy to find again. God knows I've been looking long enough to know. And he also knows I'm not choosy. A nice income, a few stocks..." She stopped herself and tugged at her jacket. "Anyway, the point is that Eden is just lucky I was home this morning when the calls came. I smoothed everything over, and we're still on. Now where is she?''

''Sleeping,'' Steve lied.

''Well, that figures, after she was up half the night terrifying my suppliers.'' Arlene reached into her pocket and pulled out a card. ''You be sure and give her this. It is absolutely the last date that I can give her for a proper fitting. After that, it's safety pins and masking tape if the gown needs altering.''

Steve studied the card as Arlene's words took hold. ''There was a headpiece in the office the day Eden and I were there. Just a little thing, some beads and pearls, a few feathers—''

''I know the one,'' Arlene said. ''Hardest number to move. Not enough height.''

''Well, hold on to it for me, will you?'' Steve smiled and slapped the card against his palm. ''And I'll make sure Eden gets this.''

When the buzzer sounded, Eden laid the storyboard on the floor beside the couch and pointed a finger at Rocky as she got to her feet. ''Stay off and I mean it,'' she warned, then pushed the intercom button. ''Who is it?''

''Delivery.'' The voice crackled and hissed, but the word was clear enough and Eden held down the button to let him in.

''Must be the editing suite,'' she said to Rocky, who was already sitting on the storyboard, washing his face. Eden blew out an exasperated breath and opened the door. After days of doodling, they both knew her idea was going nowhere. But he didn't have to rub it in.

''Eden Wells?'' The young man at the door held out a plastic pouch and a board. ''Sign here.''

With the bill signed, Eden carried the courier's envelope

to the sofa and sat down. She tore back the strip and pulled out a small blue box.

She glanced down at Rocky. "Definitely not software, and get off there." She shooed him off the board on principle, then lifted the lid. On top was a picture of George sitting outside the house, surrounded by surveyors' stakes. The caption on the bottom read, "Me in the Conservatory."

Knowing who had sent it, Eden eyed the tissue in the box. "Rocky, this is going to be bad for me, I can tell." Slowly she peeled back the tissue and blinked back tears. Why now? she wondered. When she'd almost made it through one whole hour without picking up the phone, or grabbing for her keys. Nearly sixty minutes when she hadn't found herself wandering aimlessly through the apartment, longing to climb back into the van and run, only this time not away from anything, but to something. Something magical and wonderful and too good to be true.

She lifted the headpiece out of the box, watching the tiny pearls jostle and dance. As insubstantial as a dream, she mused. And yet she held it in her hand.

Eden dared another look inside the box and saw the note. He would always leave a note, she thought and smiled as she unfolded it on her lap. "We miss you. We love you. Come home."

Home. The word sounded strange inside her head. Strange and completely right.

Eden set the box aside and grabbed for the phone. Remembering she'd unplugged it, she crawled under the table to find the jack and jammed the end in just as the buzzer sounded again.

"What now?" she said, punching the numbers into the phone as she pressed the intercom.

"Eden?"

She dropped the phone and ran out into the hall. She

heard his footsteps on the stairs—light, fast—and felt herself blush. He'd been thinking about her.

He stood now at the top of the stairs, very broad and very dark, his eyes as unreadable as the first day they'd met. But she knew the curve of his lips, the tilt of his head and the meaning of that slow, easy walk as he came toward her. He'd come to take her home.

"How did you find me?" she said, her voice no more than a whisper.

He stopped. "I'll always find you. If you want me to."

Eden nodded, aware again that he was giving her an out, letting her choose. And as she walked to meet him, Eden knew she'd made her choice. For better or worse. Forever.

He swung her up and around, then carried her back to her apartment and kicked the door closed with his foot. Noise and laughter, she thought, Steve was back.

He set her down and wrapped his arms around her, drawing her closer. "I've got a message from Arlene."

Eden moistened her lips as their hips touched and pressed. "Arlene?"

He nodded, running his hands down her back, molding her tightly to him. "Something about a fitting."

"The fit's just fine," she said, her arms weightless, drifting up to circle his neck. "Perfect, in fact."

He smiled and slid his hands up to her waist, slowly tugging her T-shirt free of her jeans. "And the caterer," he said, his fingers brushing her skin. "He wants to know about dessert."

"I like dessert," she whispered, rising up on her toes, hungry for the taste she'd missed so much. Then the words registered and she pulled back. "I canceled the caterer."

"Arlene called them back," he said, moving his hands between them and finding her belt. "Seems she didn't take you seriously."

"Oh, I'm very serious."

He pulled away and looked at her. "Are you saying you want to marry me?" She nodded but he shook his head. "I want to hear it."

Eden moistened her lips and found the words easy to say. "I love you, Steve, and I want to marry you. Today, tomorrow, I don't care when. I just know I want to be with you forever."

He lifted her T-shirt up and off. "I think September would be nice."

"In the gazebo," she murmured.

He nuzzled her neck and heard her laugh. "How long do roses bloom anyway?"

* * * * *

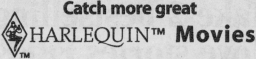 

Take 2 bestselling love stories FREE

Plus get a FREE surprise gift!

Special Limited-Time Offer

Mail to Silhouette Reader Service™

3010 Walden Avenue
P.O. Box 1867
Buffalo, N.Y. 14269-1867

YES! Please send me 2 free Silhouette Yours Truly™ novels and my free surprise gift. Then send me 4 brand-new novels every other month, which I will receive months before they appear in bookstores. Bill me at the low price of $2.90 each plus 25¢ delivery and applicable sales tax, if any.* That's the complete price, and a saving of over 10% off the cover prices—quite a bargain! I understand that accepting the books and gift places me under no obligation ever to buy any books. I can always return a shipment and cancel at any time. Even if I never buy another book from Silhouette, the 2 free books and the surprise gift are mine to keep forever.

201 SEN CH72

Name	(PLEASE PRINT)	
Address	Apt. No.	
City	State	Zip

This offer is limited to one order per household and not valid to present Silhouette Yours Truly™ subscribers. *Terms and prices are subject to change without notice. Sales tax applicable in N.Y.

USYT-98

©1996 Harlequin Enterprises Limited

International bestselling author

JOAN JOHNSTON

**continues her wildly popular Hawk's Way
miniseries with an all-new, longer-length novel**

THE SUBSTITUTE GROOM

HAWK'S WAY

August 1998

Jennifer Wright's hopes and dreams had rested on her summer wedding—until a single moment changed everything.
Including the *groom*. Suddenly Jennifer agreed to marry her
fiancé's best friend, a darkly handsome Texan she needed—
and desperately wanted—almost against her will. But U.S.
Air Force Major Colt Whitelaw had sacrificed too much to
settle for a marriage of convenience, and that made hiding
her passion all the more difficult. And hiding her biggest
secret downright impossible...

**"Joan Johnston does contemporary Westerns
to perfection."**   —*Publishers Weekly*

Available in August 1998
wherever Silhouette books are sold.

MATERNITY LEAVE

Coming September 1998

Three delightful stories about the blessings
and surprises of "Labor" Day.

TABLOID BABY by Candace Camp

She was whisked to the hospital in the nick of time....

THE NINE-MONTH KNIGHT
by Cait London

A down-on-her-luck secretary is experiencing
odd little midnight cravings....

THE PATERNITY TEST by Sherryl Woods

The stick turned blue before her
biological clock struck twelve....

*These three special women are very pregnant...and very
single, although they won't be either for too much longer,
because baby—and Daddy—are on their way!*

Available at your favorite retail outlet.

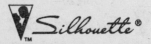